legend & lore

also by
tr rook

legend & lore

TR ROOK

Legend & Lore
by TR Rook

Published by Arctic Circle Press
www.arcticcirclepress.com

Cover designed by Tina T. Kove

ISBN ebook: 978-82-93507-25-3
ISBN print: 978-82-93507-24-6

Second edition June 2016.

table of contents

fenris forest

about the story

The forest is dark as filled with monsters.

In the hopes of gaining approval from his brother, Mihai accepts a challenge: head into Fenris Forest and retrieve a leaf from the rare Dragon's Tear tree to prove he did what he swore. But the forest is filled with monsters — and everyone's warned not go in it, because if they do not everyone comes back.

But Mihai's longing for approval trumps his fear of what lives in the forest — and he ventures inside. In there he learns that everyone was right, that Fenris Forest should be avoided — because he's attacked by one of the most dangerous creatures in there: a warg.

Mihai is certain he'll die, like so many others that have gone into the forest... but then he is unexpectedly saved, and this brings around a motion of events that will change Mihai's sheltered life forever.

chapter one
dragon's treasure

The forest loomed threateningly in front of him, enormous trees reaching high towards the sky and branches fluttering in the wind, giving off a faint sound like whispers.

It chilled Mihai to the bone but he could not back down now. He was here, he'd made that stupid bet, and he would have to take the consequences. He couldn't go back, not without proof that he'd actually been into the forest itself.

Why did I do this? he wondered to himself miserably. Oh yeah, because he'd wanted to impress not just his brother, but his brother's best friend. Maybe Flynn would actually notice him then.

Though, before Mihai had left the village, Flynn had looked at him as if he was crazy. That was not much better than not being noticed at all.

And so now he was here. Standing in front of Fenris Forest, and having no choice but to enter if there was ever any hope of being noticed in any way. A good way, at least. He just had to go into the forest, get a leaf off a rare breed of tree, and go back home.

That was his brother's challenge. And Mihai was taking it and he was going to make it. He was. Though the forest was awfully frightening.

All their lives, all everyone was told was to not go into Fenris Forest, because there lived all kinds of vile creatures. Dominating it all were the wargs. Big, wild, vicious beasts, they were said to be. Mihai desperately hoped he wouldn't be meeting one of them on his trip.

Taking a deep breath, he finally forced his feet to move. The trees loomed higher, and as he passed between the two foremost, the light immediately started to dim. Of course it got darker, Mihai hadn't expected differently with such enormous trees, but it was frightening all the same.

He couldn't deny that the forest was beautiful though. Bright green trees, the packed earth covered in fallen leaves and branches. The sky could just be glimpsed between the fluttering leaves.

No one knew exactly where to find this rare tree, with leaves the colour of silver. Only witches entered the forest, because only they had what was necessary to protect themselves against what lurked in the woods.

Mihai startled at a sound to his right, a rustling in the bushes lining the side of the path he was on. If it could be called a path, that was, with how overgrown it was.

He thought he saw a flash of grey in all the green. *It was nothing*, he told himself sternly. *Just a figment of your imagination*. He couldn't help the shivering that came over him, though, and he wrapped his arms around his torso as he pressed on.

"I can't do this," he whispered to himself, glancing around nervously. If he even found this tree, would he be able to find his way out again? Would those that lived here in the forest *let* him get out?

A flash of silver to his right and Mihai let out a gasp of surprise as he realised what it was he was seeing. The tree!

He bolted from the path, pushed away the branches in his way and stopped right in front of the tree. It was quite small though, hardly fitting to be called a tree at all. More like a big bush, he'd say, except that it had branches and those silver leaves ...

It was gorgeous. He didn't want to ruin the beauty of it by plucking a few leaves, but he had to. He had to have the proof of having been in the forest. Else he wouldn't live it down. Hraban had, according to himself, been several times inside the forest, and Mihai did not want to be a coward like everyone thought him to be.

So he reached out reluctantly and carefully plucked three leaves, tucking them neatly into the pocket of his vest. He patted his chest slightly, making sure they lay all right, then he turned to start the way back, only to stop dead.

There stood not just one, but three big, grey-furred wolves. *No, wargs*, he reminded himself. These were too big to be regular wolves. They blocked the way he'd come and Mihai didn't dare bolt further into the forest. He had no idea where he'd end up then. At the same time, there they were, right in front of him.

The one closest to him bared his teeth in a deep growl, and the one farthest back took a step forward. Mihai was terrified. All his life he'd heard of these beasts and now he was face to face with three of them. Were they going to attack? Kill him? Or possibly eat him? He shivered at the thought.

He took one cautious step back, then, as all three wolves took a step forward, the panic took him and he ran. Past the rare tree and further in. Branches hit him across the face, but he was so terrified he couldn't feel the pain.

As he was running under a tree with hanging branches that blinded him completely, his foot caught on something and he fell face first to the ground. Grass and weeds broke his fall, but fallen twigs prodded painfully against his palms and face and chest.

He lay stunned for a moment, then turned around, crawling backwards at the sight of the wargs approaching. He didn't get very far before a big rock blocked his way and he backed into it hard.

The growling got louder, the wargs were coming closer. Mihai trembled in fear. Was he going to die now? Was he never going home? No one would know what had happened to him. Everyone else who had gone missing in the Forest of Fenris had never been heard from or seen again.

At least Hraban would know he'd been into

the forest, he thought dryly. That would be a sure sign when he never came back.

Two of the wargs stopped, but the third kept advancing. Mihai's eyes were only for the big teeth that were bared: the last thing he would ever see. The thing that would kill him.

A blur of grey came from above him, and Mihai startled at the sight. There was a fourth one? Was he going to be today's dinner?

But the new warg didn't go for Mihai, it went for the approaching beast. They fell to the ground in a flurry of grey fur, bared teeth and claws. They growled and snapped after each other, but the newest arrival seemed to be winning.

Mihai curled up, wrapping his arms around his knees as he watched the fight with wide eyes.

The wargs that had hung back seemed to be hesitating for some reason. They watched the fight take place and seemed to want to join in, but they held back.

Mihai watched the fighting beasts, able to tell them apart by how the newest had more black in his fur than any of the others. It snapped after the other's throat, and barely grazed his fur. Then they rolled over, and the black-and-grey furred warg's jaws locked over the other's neck.

The grey-furred warg howled in pain, then it whimpered and carefully lowered its body as low to the ground as it could get, with its ears and tail lowered as well. The newest warg let it go, and it crept over to its two fellows before rising to its full height. The new warg stood in front of Mihai, and it seemed to be staring at the other three, who stared back a moment before taking off into the forest.

Mihai breathed out in relief, then sucked it in again as the remaining warg turned towards him. It stared at him for a moment before taking a step towards the way Mihai had come from. He then turned his head to stare at Mihai again.

Mihai blinked. It almost seemed like the beast wanted him to follow. After taking another step and look back, Mihai finally rose on shaky legs. He had to hold on to the big rock he'd been pressed against to keep his balance. Being chased by wargs really had done him in.

He startled as a furred body rubbed up against him and he looked down into the warg's eyes. Eyes that seemed more intelligent and caring than eyes of a predator should be. But it was obvious what it wanted, and Mihai tangled his fingers into the startlingly soft fur. The warg started walking and Mihai followed at its side, hand buried deep into the fur on its back.

Mihai kept glancing nervously at the big beast, but the warg just kept walking, keeping its head forward and focused on the overgrown path they were on.

And before he knew it, they were at the edge of the forest. Mihai stared around, surprised at being just where he had entered. He tightened his hand in the fur, then let go quickly as the warg curved his back slightly.

"I'm sorry, I didn't mean to ..." He shut up and pursed his lips. "I don't know why I'm apologizing. You can't understand what I'm saying anyway." But the way the big, furred head was tilted to the side and eyes trained on Mihai, he had a creeping feeling that maybe it did.

Mihai took a hesitant step backward, wanting to get home but also not quite wanting to leave the warg. It had saved his life, after all. But it was still a warg, supposed to be a savaged beast that would kill him in an instant.

"I really thank you," he mumbled, twisting his hands nervously. He felt silly, talking to an animal, but he also felt like he had to thank it somehow. "Without you, I would've... Anyway, thank you for saving my life." He turned on his heel and ran. Back to the village, to his family, to his life. Away from Fenris Forest and the kind warg that had saved him. That had led him back to the edge of the forest.

He really owed it his life.

Mihai didn't stop running until he reached the village and even then he only took a short break to get his breath back before he continued through the streets. He stopped in his tracks when he reached the square, where he saw Hraban and Flynn sitting by the fountain, joking and laughing.

Mihai felt it like a slap in the face. Here he'd been going into a forest, on a dare from his brother, where most never returned. And here they sat, laughing and joking. Weren't they worried about him at all?

Sure, he knew Hraban despised him... but Flynn, wasn't he more compassionate? Didn't he care at all either? Didn't he even feel one tiny hint of remorse?

Mihai took a step backwards, wanting to slink back home, but then something inside his mind seemed to click. Why was he backing down? He should confront them. So what if his brother sent him on a death mission? So what if he didn't care about Mihai's welfare? He should very well be shown that Mihai had survived the Forest of Fenris — and had survived it splendidly.

He forced his feet to move until he was a few feet from Hraban and Flynn. "Miss me?" he asked, and couldn't keep all of the bitterness out of his voice. Two pair of eyes turned to him in annoyance. Those eyes widened in surprise when they realized who was actually standing there.

"Been to the forest, huh?" Hraban asked mockingly. "Like you'd be so cocky if you'd been in there."

Mihai opened his pocket and pulled out the leaves. "Here's your proof. I went into the forest. I came back. Sorry to disappoint you on the last one." He turned his back on their shocked faces and walked towards home.

He took all the side streets, not wanting to meet anyone. He'd always known Hraban didn't particularly care about him... He'd never thought the dislike would be quite so drastic.

My brother hates me. The thought felt like an anvil to the gut.

It got heavier at the thought of going home. What did he really have to go home to? A sister who didn't particularly like him either and a mother who treated him like a stranger in his own home. It had always been like that: everyone else getting along perfectly, and him the odd man out. He didn't know why it was like that. He hadn't the faintest clue.

There had always been a distance between him, his mother and siblings, but after his father had died three years past, things had never been the same. When Father had died, they'd all got decidedly colder towards him, as if they blamed him for Father's death.

Mihai sighed and slowed his steps. If he was lucky, Mother would be out at one of her tea parties. If he wasn't, she would be there, waiting to descend on him like a hawk on its prey.

"You!"

Mihai startled as a hand was wrapped around his wrist. He was forcefully turned around and he managed to see the gnarled old face of the village witch before she was dragging him off somewhere. They went through two alleys and through an old, wooden door. Mihai tried to resist, but the old hands held more strength in them than he had expected, and he found that he could not break loose.

"Let me go," he said, but his voice held no force behind it. The old woman had always scared him and he did not want to see what could happen should he anger her. It was said she held considerable powers and that she could've been a great witch in the big city if she hadn't chosen to settle down here in this small, far-away village.

"Sit," the old woman ordered him, pushing him towards a rocking chair in the corner of the little room.

Mihai rubbed his arm, knowing he would have bruises as a result of her crushing grip come morning. He reluctantly obeyed, sitting down gingerly in the rocking chair. "What do you want with me?" he asked softly, resigning himself to his fate. It didn't look like she was going to allow him to leave anytime soon.

"Where did you get the Dragon's Treasure?" Her voice was hoarse, but intense and demanding an answer. It was obvious she was a woman who was used to being obeyed.

Her question was confusing though. "The what?" Mihai really had no idea what she was talking about. Dragon's Treasure? Dragons were said to live on the other side of the Black Mountains, but no one in the village had ever seen one. They were myth, and perhaps they were everywhere as well, but at least they were said to live across the mountains. He'd never heard of a dragon's treasure and Mihai would never have anything like that. Where would he have acquired it?

"The leaves!" Her hand shot out and snagged the leaves Mihai still held in his other hand.

"No, don't" Mihai reached for them, but they were already out of his reach, clasped firmly in her wrinkled old fingers.

"These leaves are called Dragon's Treasure," she started explaining to him while settling her old body into the other rocking chair in the room. "Powerful leaves they are, if one knows how to use them correctly."

"I don't," Mihai assured her, hoping that that was what she wanted to hear. "I've never even seen such leaves before. I just went into the forest on a dare from my brother..."

"You went into the forest?"

Mihai nodded. "I just plucked a few leaves off the small tree to show Hraban and Flynn that I'd been in there. I wasn't going to do anything with them, I swear." Somehow, he had a feeling he was in trouble. It was just a few leaves though, so he didn't really see the problem, but obviously there was one or he wouldn't be here inside the village witch's home.

"You obviously came out alive." It wasn't a question, so Mihai felt like he didn't actually have to answer. He felt like the less he said now, the better off he would be. "So you know nothing about the Dragon's Treasure?"

Mihai nodded his head quickly. "No, nothing, ma'am."

She lent forward, eyes intent on Mihai. "Only witches can pluck a leaf off a Dragon tree. That is why the leaves are called the Dragon's Treasure, because the tree guards them jealously until a real witch, or one with witch potential, comes along to pluck them."

Mihai blinked at the explanation she'd given him, slowly taking it in. Then the meaning of it sank in and he shot to his feet. "You're quite mistaken," he told her, voice shaking just the tiniest bit. "I'm quite ordinary. Less than, even. I have to get home now."

"Wait!"

Mihai stopped, even if he didn't want to. The implications of her words... he couldn't take them in.

"Here are your leaves. Take good care of them." She thrust the leaves into his hand, and then turned to walk across the room. Mihai was at the door with his hand on the knob before she spoke again. "It seems you have never been told. You should ask your mother about your real origins."

Mihai slammed the door closed behind him, his heart beating double the pace it normally did. He couldn't help that her words stuck in his mind, going around and around in circles.

Either the old witch was lying... or Mother was keeping a big secret from him.

Mihai was finding it difficult to forget the old witch's words. Something had always been off between himself and the rest of the family, besides his father. Maybe what the witch was talking about was the answer ...

But Mihai did not know how to bring it up. He did not go down for dinner because he knew perfectly well how that would be. Instead he snuck down to the kitchen later in the evening to make his own food. He preferred that, else he would only be met by stony silence at the dinner table.

And now he was in bed, unable to sleep. The leaves lay on the bedside table, and they shone silver by the light of the moon through the window. They really were beautiful, but looking at them also brought back the witch's words. He didn't like the implications of them, but at the same time he burned to know.

Mihai tossed and turned, but was too restless to sleep. He threw the covers off and sat up. He stared at his clothes lying neatly folded on a chair for a moment, then quickly pulled them on. Maybe a night-time stroll would settle his mind.

He walked as silently as possible through the house, and the door only creaked slightly as he pulled it open only enough for him to slip through. He took a deep breath as he stood on the stairs, feeling better already in the fresh air, then he went down the steps and started his trek through the village.

He didn't really have any specific thought of where to go, but eventually he realised that he was walking towards the forest. He halted for a moment, then asked himself why. The only good thing that had happened to him lately had been there, earlier in the day. The warg that had saved him and brought him back to the edge of the forest...

Maybe he'd see the beast again. He found that he actually wanted to. The warg had saved him, then helped him. It was more than anyone else did nowadays. After the trouble it had gone through to save Mihai and help him back, he felt certain that it wouldn't harm him.

But it was in the middle of the night, he thought gloomily as he saw the forest ahead. Certainly even wolves were asleep at this time of night, especially when it had gone to the trouble of saving him earlier in the day.

He stood only a few feet from the enormous trees, gazing into the darkness ahead. The moon had lit up his way there, but inside the forest it was pitch dark. The trees shut out the bright moonlight, making the forest seem even scarier than ever.

Mihai did not want to venture in there. *This was a stupid idea*. He should go back home, get some sleep, and come back tomorrow. He'd feel better in the daylight, certainly. At least he'd stand a better chance of meeting the black-and-grey furred warg again.

He bit his lips, hesitating as he started to turn around. He squinted, trying to see if he could glimpse anything behind the tree line, but it really was too dark for him. He could see nothing and anything he thought he saw was his eyes playing tricks on him.

He turned with a sigh, but stopped dead, his

heart galloping in his chest, as he noticed someone standing there. "Hraban?" he asked, blinking his eyes in surprise at seeing his older brother standing there. "What're you doing here?"

"Finally dealing with you." Hraban's voice was chillier than the frost covering the ground at winter. Something gleamed at his side from the moonlight, and when Hraban took a step forward Mihai saw what it was he was holding.

A knife. One of those big ones that were used in the kitchen to cut up the meat.

"What are you doing?" Mihai started backing away nervously.

"You've always been a thorn in our side," Hraban spoke. "Because of Father, we had to live with you. Because of his wish, and because you've always been normal, we've let you be. But those leaves you got... Apparently those aren't easily acquired, or so Mother says."

Mihai felt his chest tightening in apprehension.

"Apparently you're of the same ilk as your mother, after all."

"We have the same mother," Mihai argued.

Hraban laughed coldly at that. "No, we don't, you little bastard. Your mother stopped by here about twenty years ago and seduced Father. But when she'd born you, their bastard child, she left you at our doorstep to take care of. Father was too kind not to take you in. But now that Father is dead, we don't want witches in our house."

Mihai blinked rapidly, trying to avoid the tears welling up. It was no good though, they came anyway. He'd been lied to all his life. He could understand Mother and his siblings, but even Father had...

How could Father have lied him to? Father, who was the only one who cared about him.

"I have to do this, Mihai. You weren't even supposed to be born. I'm just setting things right."

Mihai drew in a shaky breath, eyes wide as he watched Hraban approach. He had nowhere to go. The dark forest loomed behind him, and if he ran to either side Hraban would catch up to him. He'd always been faster, and in their childhood he'd always used it to his advantage. Mihai didn't have an advantage of any sort. He'd always been small and weak, and even his sister had been able to take him down when they were still children.

"Hraban!" someone shouted, the voice carrying loud and clear. Mihai recognized that voice and drew in a shaky breath. It was Flynn. What was Flynn doing here? Was he helping Hraban in his task of getting rid of Mihai, the bastard child of their father?

Hraban turned his head sharply to watch Flynn come running towards them. His lips pressed together into a thin line, and Mihai understood that Flynn was not with him in this. Hraban was displeased to see his best friend.

"Hraban! Have you gone nuts?" But Flynn was to far away and Hraban was too close to Mihai. He realized it just a second before Hraban jumped on him, the knife burrowing painfully into Mihai's side. Mihai screamed. Never had he felt pain like this... even that one time as a little boy when he'd fallen and hit his head on a rock couldn't even compare.

He screamed again as the knife was twisted inside the wound, then abruptly drawn out. Hraban stood up on his knees, holding the knife with both hands above him. His eyes glinted in the light of the moon and Mihai saw the madness in them clearly for just one second. Then Hraban made to thrust the knife into Mihai's gut—

—only to be tumbled off of Mihai's body by a big, furred wolf. It growled deep in its throat as it bit down over Hraban's wrist. The warg shook its head back and forth, ignoring Hraban who was wailing in pain, until the knife fell to the ground.

But the warg was not letting Hraban off the hook that easily. Once it let go of his arm, it shoved him face first into the ground with its big, wide front paws. It stepped on him, holding him down. Painfully, to judge by Hraban's groans.

The warg turned its head then and looked Mihai straight in the eye. Mihai was breathing heavily, erratically, and all he wanted was to pass out, but he couldn't look away from those canine, yet quite warm and intelligent, eyes.

It was the warg from earlier. His warg. Yet again it had come to his rescue. Mihai couldn't help but wonder what was so special about him, to have one of the feared wargs as a rescuer.

"Mihai!" Strong hands touched him, felt for his wound and pressed against it once they found it. Mihai let out a pained sob, his vision blurring. He could still see the warg, but it wasn't looking at him any longer. It was regarding the one standing above Mihai, and Mihai turned his head slowly to follow its gaze.

Flynn was bending over him, worry written

all over his handsome face as he pressed his hands against Mihai's injured side.

"Hurts," Mihai whispered, his vision blurring even more at the pain that brought. He turned his head back the other way, looking at the warg still pressing Hraban into the ground. The furred head bent slightly towards him, and those eyes met Mihai's. It was the last thing Mihai saw before all went black.

When he woke, it was pitch dark. He could see nothing. Afraid, he scrambled to get a hold of something, only to be stilled by a strong hand pressing him back down into what he realized was a soft bed.

"You need to lay still. Your wound might be wrapped up, but too much moving around and you will ruin all the hard work put into it."

Mihai frowned at the foreign voice. Last he knew, Flynn and Hraban had been the only men around. "Flynn?" he couldn't help but ask, making certain, but he knew Flynn's voice too well after having been so infatuated with the man that he knew it could not be him.

A soft laugh greeted that question. "My name is Garrick. The one that helped you, the one named Flynn, is fast asleep in his own room."

Mihai let the words sink in. "I am in Flynn's house?"

"He certainly could not bring you home, could he?" Garrick's voice was now tinged with sadness.

"No," Mihai whispered brokenly. "He couldn't." He probably couldn't go home anymore. Even if Hraban had acted all on his own, neither Sister nor Mother would take Mihai's story over Hraban, not after what had been revealed. "What happened to Hraban?"

"Nothing too bad," came the reply from his side. Garrick had to be sitting in a chair at his bedside. "A few scratches, a bite. Nothing much. He'll live. Though he got a real scare. I doubt he'll ever go close to the forest again." The voice was tinged with laughter now.

Mihai didn't know what to feel about Hraban being all right. He didn't know what he'd be feeling if he hadn't been either. His thoughts were a jumbled mess, and he didn't even know where to start processing them. "Am I going to be alright?" he asked, feeling a dull throbbing at his side where Hraban had buried the knife.

"The old witch fixed you up once Flynn got you back to the village," Garrick replied softly.

"You'll need to heal, but you'll be alright."

Mihai didn't even know what he felt about that. He would be all right... but he had no home to return to. He probably couldn't even stay in the village. Not if he didn't want a repeat of what had happened. He knew his brother well enough to know that if Hraban had decided on something, he wouldn't stop until he'd achieved it.

"Who are you?" He had never heard Garrick's voice before, of that he was certain, so it was odd that he was sitting at Mihai's bedside in the middle of the night and knew of what had transpired.

"I told you, didn't I? I'm Garrick."

"You told me your name, but I still don't know *who* you are," Mihai pressed, finding it easier to have his mind on Garrick than focus on everything else vying for attention.

Footsteps sounded inside the house and Garrick rose in one swift, smooth motion. His clothes rustled slightly, but other than that Mihai heard no sound from him. "That is my cue to leave. Get well, Mihai, and we'll soon see each other again." He swooped down and pressed a soft kiss to Mihai's lips, and then he was at the window, drawing the curtains apart.

Mihai only saw him silhouetted by the moonlight for a second then he jumped out and was gone.

chapter two
witch

The man left not a moment too soon, it would seem, because the door creaked open only moments later. Mihai could not see who it was, because he didn't dare move after Garrick had warned him about it reopening his wound. Someone was coming into the room and closing the door after themselves, but a small lamp lit up and soon Flynn's face came into sight. "You're awake." Flynn sat himself down in the chair Garrick must've been sitting in and put the lit lamp on the bedside table. "How're you feeling?"

"Not so bad," Mihai replied cautiously. A day ago this would've been a dream being in Flynn's house and having Flynn sit by his bed. Having Flynn notice him in any way would've been a dream come true. But now...

Flynn might've helped him after Hraban had stabbed him, but he certainly hadn't tried to stop him going into the forest to begin with. He and Hraban had been joking and laughing and having a merry good time when Mihai came back. He hadn't seemed to care that most people never came back when they ventured inside the forest.

Flynn watched him for a moment, then sighed and bent his head. "I want to apologise, Mihai." His voice was low, and he raked one hand through his dark hair. "I should've realised sooner that Hraban would go to such measures."

"You couldn't know," Mihai mumbled. "It didn't strike him until I came back from the forest with the Dragon's Treasure earlier today."

"The day before last, you mean," Flynn commented. "You've been unconscious for the better part of a day."

Mihai turned wide eyes on the older man. "What? How is that possible?"

Flynn looked sheepish. "I had to call the village witch. I didn't know what to do with you. The fever caught you, see. She gave you something to drink and said you would be sleeping through the worst of the pain. Other than that, I don't know what she did. She didn't want to tell me."

So for a day he'd been unconscious... a whole day where Hraban probably had been up and about, laying more plans for how to get rid of him.

"I really am sorry." Flynn put his hand on Mihai's shoulder, trying to be consoling, but all Mihai wanted was to jerk away. He didn't though, but only because he didn't want to disturb his healing wound, he wanted to get well quickly. He obviously had to leave the village, there was no other option.

"You weren't sorry when I first went into the forest," Mihai snapped bitterly, turning his head away. "I'm tired. Do you mind?"

Flynn stood up slowly, but he hesitated for a moment. For what, Mihai did not know and did not care. Flynn grabbed the light and made for the door, and the darkness fell over the room once again, snuffing his infatuation with Flynn along with the light.

Mihai woke periodically throughout the day, but almost immediately fell asleep again. When he next woke up properly, it was dark outside again. And quiet. Very quiet.

Feeling another presence in the room with him, he eagerly turned his head, hoping to see the mysterious Garrick. But the curtains were parted now, and the sparse moonlight shone through enough to show that it wasn't Garrick, but the old witch, sitting in the chair.

Her gnarled, wrinkled face was facing him, and het deep-sunken eyes were locked on his face. "Good, you're awake," she croaked. "Come on, we have little time." She got her small, crooked body out of the chair with an ease he never would've believed, then preceded to draw the covers off of him.

The room wasn't chilly, but it felt like it when the warmth of the covers was taken away. Mihai quickly made sure he was wearing clothes, but found he lacked a shirt. Which was expected, since they'd have had to dress the wound, and a shirt would've been in the way.

"Come on. You should be good for walking a little, I'd say."

Mihai sat up slowly, trying not to move his upper body too much. The old woman held out a tunic for him and Mihai slowly worked it over his shoulders and down to cover his torso. She was holding a belt next, but instead of giving it to him she was stuffing it into a small pack.

"You cannot wear this," she answered his puzzled frown. "It would hurt your injured side. But you can wear *this*." And she held out a thick winter coat—*his* winter coat.

"You've been to my home?" he asked in wonder.

"Had to get your stuff, didn't I?" She closed the pack and put it over her shoulder. She looked fragile enough for it to crush her, but she seemed to hold it with ease. "I didn't get a warm welcome though. You don't even get a goodbye. But it is as expected." She said it so matter-of-factly it almost didn't sting. "Now come on, boy, we have to hurry." And she ushered him out of the room. "Be quiet; don't want to wake up your knight in shining armour."

"He is not my knight in shining armour," Mihai murmured. If anyone was his knight in shining armour, it had to be four-legged and covered in black-and-grey fur.

They walked silently through Flynn's small home, and Mihai breathed out a sigh of relief as they came out into the streets. Only then, when he was safely out, did he feel the slight throbbing at his side. It didn't hurt exactly, but it was uncomfortable. He would endure it for as long as he had to.

Mihai wanted to know where they were going, but he didn't dare ask. She looked so serious, so grim, that he didn't know what to think. He eventually recognised his surrounding though. They were leaving the village and walking towards the forest.

His side was starting to sting, but Mihai kept quiet. Instead he just held a hand lightly over the bandage, at least keeping it in place in case this hurried walking was too much for it.

When they were well away from the village, the old woman stopped. Mihai stopped as well, his breathing more laboured than normal because of his stinging side. He heard her whisper something, and for a moment he thought it was to him, before she held her hand out and it blazed up into a bright blue flame, hovering mere inches from her palm.

"Witchfire," she told him, almost gruffly, and then she was moving forward again. Mihai heaved a sigh and followed, not wanting to be left behind without any light, without anywhere to go.

The forest was coming into view, and it was coming closer and closer. Mihai squinted, certain he saw something... and there it was, a light. This flame was dark orange and decidedly normal. Someone was standing there, just outside the edge of the forest, holding a lantern.

Mihai hurried his steps so that he came up on the side of the old witch. He glanced at her, seeing her face set in determination. They slowly reached the person holding the lantern. He held the lantern in one hand and a shovel in the other. Behind him stood a big, dark horse. It seemed black, but it could have been of a lighter colour.

Mihai's eyes landed on the shovel again, following it down. He gasped, reeling back. His side stung worse, and he curled his arm around it, righting himself.

A grave. There, at the man's side, was a freshly dug grave. It wasn't big, but it was deep and would definitely fit a human.

Mihai reeled back again when the blue witchlight suddenly went out. Staring between the two, he felt dread settle in his stomach. There was one grave, they were three people ... surely one of them would end up in that grave. And Mihai had a sinking feeling he knew who would.

He started backing away, arm still curled around his injured side.

"Stop it!" the witch snapped and Mihai stopped in his tracks. "This has to be done, boy. It's too late for another course of action. It's the only way."

Mihai glanced at the silent stranger, seeing that he had his jaws clenched tightly and looking gloomier by the second. Who was this man? How did he know the old witch? She was well known not to keep in contact with anyone, unless someone was sick and needed her help.

"I'm doing it, Garrick," she said, stepping closer to Mihai.

Mihai's eyes flew from her to the man at her words. This was the mysterious Garrick?

Then the old, wrinkled hand settled on his forehead and for one split second Mihai wondered what she was up to, then... pain like he'd never imagined. He screamed and felt his knees hit the ground... He remembered nothing more.

Mihai woke to a strange feeling of being in motion. Blinking his eyes open, he instantly had to close them again as the daylight burned his eyes.

How much time had he actually spent asleep the last few days?

Then it dawned on him that he was alive... and that the last thing he remembered was excruciating pain.

He inched his eyes up slowly, letting them get used to the bright light of day. The first thing he noticed was that he was above ground, and that his cheek was pressed against a warm, lightly-furred neck.

Pushing himself up, he realised he was atop a horse. He almost lost his balance upon that shock, but a steady hand was there to right him again.

Mihai looked down at that tanned hand and followed the arm upwards... and found himself staring into the worried face of the silent man from last night. The one she'd called Garrick...

"You're Garrick?" he asked, wanting to make sure it really was the same man that had been sitting at his bedside, laughing and being cheery and ... kissing Mihai in parting. He could feel his cheeks heat at *that* thought.

"I am." He had strange eyes, Mihai thought, but couldn't quite pinpoint where he'd seen such eyes before. But they were sincere, Mihai was certain of that. Besides those strange eyes, Garrick had a square face with just a hint of stubble. His hair was dark brown and it curled against his neck and over his ears, though it wasn't overly long.

Mihai cast a look around, seeing that they were passing through a forest. Fenris Forest, it had to be. There were no other forests around. "What... happened?" He wasn't sure he wanted to know the answer, but the old witch was not to be seen, and as there had been a grave...

"You've got witch potential," Garrick started, "but are too old to be able to use your long dormant powers. When a potential witch reaches a certain age without being trained, the powers... lock themselves and the potential witch is not able to draw from them anymore. Not ever."

Mihai stared down at the man. He wasn't looking at Mihai any longer, his eyes all for the road ahead of them. And it really was a road, not the overgrown path in the forest around Mihai's village.

Something wasn't quite right ... when he focused on the man it was like he could hear something beating. Like a heart ... like he could hear the man's heart beating. "What have you done to me?" he asked panicked, clutching a hand to his chest, over his own heart, beating in the exact same rhythm as this man's. If it was indeed his heart he was hearing. It certainly was something that was beating inside his head.

Those strange eyes, seeming to glow almost yellow in the sunlight, turned to him again. "A witch can transfer her own powers into a potential, which basically gets things going. You're coming into your powers."

Mihai frowned, not wanting to process that. "What about the old woman? Where is she?"

The eyes turned sad. "When a witch transfers her own power it kills her. She rests peacefully now, content with what she has achieved."

"Achieved?"

"Unleashing your powers," Garrick said matter-of-factly. "They are manifesting in you now and once they have, you will be able to learn. You'll be what you were born to be a witch."

Mihai didn't like that. All his life Mother had been feeding them all gruesome, wicked tales of witches. She had hated them. But then again, she'd also hated Mihai ... and if what Hraban had revealed was true, then Father had had an affair with a witch. An affair that had ended in Mihai. Probably bringing Mother's hatred to life in the first place. Because she'd always been quite possessive and controlling over Father. Him having had an affair must've stung her quite nicely.

"So does that mean I'm going to be hearing everyone's heartbeat?" he asked dejectedly. "Because it is rather annoying."

Garrick's head whipped toward him. "You hear my heartbeat?"

Mihai nodded mutely.

"I didn't know it went both ways..." He was mumbling to himself, but Mihai caught it nonetheless.

"Both ways?" he asked sharply. "Do you feel mine?"

It was Garrick's turn to nod. "But only yours. And you'll only hear mine."

"What does *that* mean?" Mihai wasn't sure he could take much more. His mind felt full, like there wasn't any more space for anything else. He didn't know if he could take much else happening to him either. His life was turning upside down, and he had no idea what exactly was going on or how it would continue.

"We're bonded," Garrick replied, voice low. "I am your familiar."

Mihai looked at him blankly, not knowing what that word was supposed to mean. "I don't understand," he said when Garrick made no move to look at him again or continue speaking.

"Neither do I, really," Garrick replied.

"Normally it's common for witches to have a familiar, one whom they're bound to completely. A familiar aids and helps his witch. But I'm not much of a help when it comes to magic, because besides being able to shift, I have none."

"Shift?" Mihai stared down at him, eyes wide. "You're a shifter?"

A slight nod of the head and a brief glance of strange eyes was all the answer he got. Strange eyes... Mihai frowned in thought, suddenly realising what Garrick seemed to be waiting on him to figure out. Strange eyes... strange *canine* eyes. Just like the eyes of the warg that had saved his life twice. "You're him," he whispered. "The warg that's been saving me lately."

Garrick nodded again.

"Then those other three, they're shifters too? So why did they try to kill me?"

"They sensed that you are a witch, but they hadn't sense enough to realise that your powers were dormant," Garrick explained. "But then those three are idiots. That's not ever going to change."

"But how did you"

"I sensed you the moment you entered the forest," Garrick broke him off. "This forest is my home more than where my parents live. I know it well, and sometimes it talks to me."

"Then maybe you have some magic, after all?" Mihai asked lightly. "Because I've never heard of a forest speaking to anyone before."

Garrick smiled briefly at that. "The Forest of Fenris is not like any other forest. The spirits of our forefathers reside here. They are the forest. That's why when bad people come in here, they never come out. When those that are born a warg go in they are led to our settlement. When witches come in, they are either left in peace if they do not come too close, or attacked, just as you were."

"I do not want to be a witch," Mihai said dejectedly. "I do not know *how* to be one."

"You will learn." Garrick smiled at him. "But first your wound has to heal. Besides, your powers need time to settle. You can't learn when they're still in turmoil from being woken after having been dormant for so long."

Mihai bent his head, staring down at the horse's neck. It really was black, as it had seemed last night. A hand settled on his knee then, startling Mihai. He glanced up, meeting Garrick's eyes again. "I have to warn you," Garrick said, eyes intense. "You won't get the best of welcomes in our village."

"Why not?"

"Well... our rule is not to mingle with outsiders, especially not witches." Garrick's hand squeezed Mihai's knee slightly harder than he probably meant.

"Why not witches?" Mihai asked curiously, trying not to wince at the grip on his knee.

"Because once, a long time ago, one of us was bonded to a witch. That witch abused the bond. It has made them all wary, even centuries after it happened."

"But you don't share their view, do you?" Mihai nibbled his lip nervously. Garrick seemed to like him all right, and he'd known about Mihai's potential all along. He couldn't mind their bonding, could he?

"No, I don't. I think it's foolish. One bad case and we're supposed to shun everyone but our own kind? It's really quite ridiculous."

Mihai felt relieved at hearing Garrick was not hostile towards witches, though he really should've known. Garrick had been nothing but kind to him from the beginning.

"Here we are," Garrick said then. "Home, sweet home." Mihai didn't miss the sarcasm in his voice at that. He tore his eyes away from Garrick and looked ahead. The forest gave way to open land covered in huts and cabins and small houses; fields upon fields where people were already out working.

It was beautiful, but as Garrick and Mihai closed in on the village more and more people seemed to notice them, and they all stared from one to the other. Mihai shifted self-consciously. Not one of these people were smiling. Their faces were set in disapproving grimaces.

"Best to get this over with right away," Garrick murmured to himself, then led the horse towards the biggest house, standing majestically in what was supposed to be a square. "Come on, get down."

Mihai scrambled down from the horse, but the wound in his side decided to make itself known then and he stumbled. Garrick caught him smoothly, but that too jostled his wound and Mihai gasped in pain.

"Easy there." Garrick got him properly set down on his feet, but held on to Mihai's shoulder until the pain subsided.

"Thank you," Mihai mumbled sheepishly, feeling his cheeks heat up.

"I know you're in pain," Garrick replied softly. "Anyone would be with a knife wound in their side. You're going to rest soon, but I think it best if we get this over with first." He motioned to the house they were standing in front of.

"What's in there?" Mihai asked curiously, sensing Garrick's dread.

"Hell." Garrick's jaw clenched. "Also known as my parents."

Garrick dreaded the confrontation he knew was coming, but things had gone this far—he had no other choice but to bring Mihai home with him.

Mihai certainly couldn't have stayed in the village, not with a brother wanting him dead. And certainly not after the witch had gone. Mihai's family would have found some way to pin it on him, if they hadn't already. But Mihai was not going back there. *That,* Garrick was going to make sure of.

He made sure to be a step ahead of Mihai as they entered, wanting to spare him the whole confrontation, but knowing he couldn't do that. Too long Mihai had been kept from a lot of important information about his life. All Garrick could do now was make sure nothing else was kept from him ever again.

So Mihai was here with him, whether Garrick

liked it or not.

They crossed the hallway, and Garrick pushed open the double doors leading into the salon, where his parents spent most of their time and where they entertained guests. Not that this would be much entertainment.

As he'd told Mihai outside, it would be hell.

"Garrick!" His mother stood up in a rustle of skirts, then stopped short once her eyes landed on Mihai. "What's that?"

"That's a human, Mother," Garrick replied tersely.

"And a witch," she snapped.

His father stood up as well, standing straight at his wife's side. "Why are you bringing a witch into our midst?" he questioned. "You know our rules."

"He can't go back home," Garrick started to explain. "He has no proper family, no friends. He was almost murdered. I had no choice."

"If you so cared about his fate, you could've taken him to another village. Villages welcome witches, because most don't have one. We don't want that kind around here. Around us."

"He's staying with me, at *my* cabin," Garrick told her. "He's hurt and needs rest. And that's that."

"Garrick" His mother's voice was threatening. "What if he bonds with any of us?" she snapped. "What then, Garrick?"

"You don't have to worry about anyone being bonded to him," Garrick replied stonily, "because someone already is."

It took them both a second to figure it out, but once they did shock was written all over their faces. Rustling skirts was the only warning he got before he was slapped hard across the face, long nails scratching his cheek.

"You low excuse for a —"

Father stepped forward, taking a hold of her shoulder and effectively breaking off the tirade Garrick knew was coming. His face was set in stone when he turned to face Garrick again. "You need to leave. Take your witch with you. We will talk about this at a later date. This discussion is not over."

Garrick stared his father in the eye for a long moment, then he turned on his heels and ushered Mihai with him outside. The young man was paler than he'd been when they'd gone inside. "My cabin is close to the forest. It won't take us long to get there." He helped Mihai back up into the saddle, then grabbed the reins and led the horse along the way leading right.

His little cabin was not remotely close to the main road into the forest. He'd made sure of that when he'd had it built. It lay so that he didn't see the road at all, and so that almost the entire village was out of sight of it.

He had no love for the village or the people living there. All his life he'd grown up with strict parents, who expected only the best. From the very start he'd not been what they had wanted. He had always been an outsider, far more interested in books than expectations.

Far too interested in the world to bother with the prejudiced people in the village. And he'd especially always been interested in witches. Now he had one right here, one that he was bound too. Garrick had always wanted to be bound to a witch, to be able to actually do some good with his life somewhere else. He loved the Forest of Fenris, but not even that could keep him here.

His cabin came into sight and he hurried his steps. He needed to get Mihai into bed. The man should've never been out of it. But it had been absolutely necessary. Hopefully his recovery would take only a little longer. They'd found each other, though, so they had all the time in the world.

Garrick sat out on the stairs, soaking up the sun and trying his hand at carving. He was not a very good carver, but it was something he enjoyed twiddling with from time to time.

Two days had gone by since he'd returned, and he had still heard nothing from either of his parents. That wasn't exactly unexpected, but considering the circumstances, he was a bit surprised. Then again, no one detested witches more in the village than his parents. They didn't know that Mihai wasn't a witch yet. They only felt his power, and it was quite some power he radiated — it was throbbing and pulsing.

Garrick wasn't sure if it was because it hadn't settled yet, or if Mihai was simply that strong. He'd never felt this kind of power from the village witch, but she'd been old and weary, her body not able to handle as much. She might've been stronger in her younger days. She'd never told him, and Garrick had not known her long enough to ask.

Two years they'd been acquainted and she still hadn't told him her name. The only thing he had from her was the memories of talks in the dark, walks in the forest... and two books she'd wanted Mihai to have. Garrick hadn't given them to him yet. He'd wait until Mihai was healthy and ready to deal with it.

Though at the rate the wound was healing, that would be sooner rather than later. It was healing unnaturally fast, that wound. He was not sure if it was something the witch had done to it, or if it was Mihai's own magic doing the trick. It might be neither, maybe he was just a fast healer. But not even wargs healed that quickly...

Then again, the only witch Garrick had ever known hadn't exactly been forthcoming with information. Sure, she'd told him plenty, but nothing that would help now. Garrick had never expected to bond to a witch, and even though he'd always been curious... bonding was the one thing the old witch had refused to talk about.

Garrick had a sinking feeling she'd once been bonded and that it had ended badly. Either the bond had broken, which should be possible according to a few books he'd got his hands on through the years, or else her familiar had died.

"Hi, Garrick!"

Garrick's head shot up and as he saw three men walking towards his cabin he silently berated himself for not sensing them approaching sooner. Especially as they were three people he wanted nothing to do with. He put his knife and wood down, then stood up. He did not want to meet them sitting. Brand had enough of a better-than-thou attitude already. "What do you want, Brand?" he asked coldly.

"Is it true you've got a witch here?" Brand looked around as if expecting to see said witch appear. "The whole village is talking about it."

"The village can stop their gossiping and leave me to lead my own life," Garrick told him stonily.

"So it is true?" Brand's eyes burned the exact same mix of orange and yellow as his wolf-form. That was the disadvantage of being a shifter: the eyes always gave it away. "Everybody speaks of how you came walking into town with a young man riding your horse."

"I have no interest in hearing about this week's gossip. Get lost, Brand." He spared a cold glance to Brand's two buddies as well, wanting all three of them off his property right this second.

"Don't tell me to get lost!" Brand snapped. "You are the one breaking our rules!"

"Why are you suddenly so dead-set in following rules?" Garrick whirled back around to face him. "You and I have broken almost every rule throughout the years! Or have you forgotten that? Just like you've forgotten how inseparable we were as children?"

Brand's face had got angrier and angrier as Garrick spoke, and when he finished he was clenching his jaw so tight Garrick worried he'd break his teeth. "I do not know what you're talking about," he got out, anger pulsing through the whole man.

"Good thing one of us still does," Garrick replied icily, turning around to go back inside. He only managed a step before he was thrown to the ground by a big, furred body. He landed painfully against the wooden steps, grunting as he had his breath knocked out of him.

He managed to get his breath back a moment later and instantly shifted. He twisted around, jaws snapping after Brand's foot. Brand jumped off him, down to the ground, but Garrick went after him. Brand was not getting away from this, assaulting him on his own property.

They rolled over, fighting for dominance. Brand almost got the better off him a couple of times, but Garrick had always been the bigger, stronger one. Eventually, he got the upper hand. He kept Brand pinned to the ground, locking his jaws over his neck. Hard enough for it to hurt, but not enough to draw blood.

Brand subsided, and Garrick eventually let him go. He stepped back, covering the stairs leading up to his cabin, growling low in his throat. Brand growled back, but then turned tail and ran for the village. Evert and Joos glanced at him once, and then they too shifted and ran after Brand, soon disappearing around the bend in the road.

When they were finally gone, Garrick shifted back to human form. He turned to go back up the stairs, but stopped short upon seeing Mihai stand in the door. He wasn't as pale as he had been. His cheeks were getting their colour back. He looked good. Really good, if a bit startled.

"Did you see all that?" Garrick asked him softly. Mihai nodded slightly, opening the door further. Garrick put one foot on the step, then changed his mind. "Are you feeling all right?"

"Yeah, much better, thank you."

"I'm going into the village for a bit. Will you be alright on your own for a little?"

Mihai nodded, but started nibbling his lip nervously. "Will you be long?"

"Not at all." Garrick shook his head. "I'll be back in a moment." He smiled, then turned and started walking.

"What are you going to do in the village?" Mihai called after him, voice soft but strong.

"Talk to my parents." Garrick clenched his jaw and balled his fists, then resumed walking steadfastly. He had to get this confrontation over with and then he needed to leave.

chapter three
escape

Garrick threw open the door to his parents' salon and went inside, eyes instantly landing on them. They stared back for a second, then they both stood up, turning to face him. "Where's your witch?" his mother asked.

"Not here," Garrick replied calmly, knowing it would be best if he at least could stay calm and rational.

"Good. I don't want him anywhere near here. Even your cabin is too near, though you made sure to have it built a good distance away." She glared at him, arms crossed over her chest.

Garrick ignored her words, instead turning to his father. "I came here to tell you that I will be leaving."

"To get rid of the witch?" he questioned.

"To be rid of this place," Garrick replied

stonily. "I have never belonged here, so my witch and I will soon be gone."

"Good," his mother snarled.

"Now wait a minute!" his father interrupted his mother, and Garrick felt a flicker of hope. Would Father finally stand up for him, would he really acknowledge him? Or just say that he would miss him? Garrick had always felt like he'd never been good enough for his parents, that no matter what he did it was never good enough. So eventually he'd just stopped caring, and done what made him happy. "You can't leave," Father spoke. "Who will take over being the head of the village if you go? You are our only child. We cannot let the duty pass to another family—it has been ours for generations."

Garrick clenched his teeth. So much for that hope. He hadn't really expected it, but it hurt all the same that his father was thinking about nothing but himself and the family name. "I've made my decision," Garrick said, voice tight. "I'm leaving. That's that."

"So just leave," his mother snapped. "You're no good for us anyway." His father stood at her side, face as stony as ever. Garrick knew he'd never get any recognition, any acceptance from them. So why even bother trying to reason? They'd never listen to what he had to say anyway.

He turned on his heels and walked briskly back outside. He jumped down the steps, shifted in mid-spring and as he hit the ground on all fours, he sprinted straight towards the forest. He ran past the tree line and continued, dodging low hanging branches and jumping over bushes. He ran until he had no breath left. When he finally stopped, on the outskirts of a clearing covered in soft, green grass, he was heaving for breath. He shifted back to his human form and collapsed on the ground, rolling over so that he lay flat on his back.

His chest rose and fell in fast motion, and he put his hands over his face, partly from protection from the sun, partly because he was trying not to break down. He didn't know why he was this upset; he already knew his parents didn't care. Maybe it was just because it had been proven once and for all.

A twig breaking close by had him up in a sitting position, and he blinked against the sun as he saw a warg standing at the other side of the clearing. A familiar warg at that. His stomach churned at the thought of Brand seeing his little breakdown. "What do you want?" he called out.

Brand seemed to be hesitating, his head swinging from the path he was on to Garrick and back again. Garrick frowned as Brand took a cautious step towards him. Usually he would've come without hesitation—he never let a chance to taunt Garrick get away from him.

Brand stopped several feet from Garrick and shifted back to human form. His mouth was pressed together, and he looked both resigned and determined. "You should leave, Garrick," he spoke quietly. "Don't wait. No one is happy about you having a witch in your house and they plan on doing something about it..."

Garrick's brain churned. Was Brand... warning him? "What are they planning to do?" he asked gruffly. "Mihai hasn't done anything but rest in my cabin."

"He's a witch," Brand stressed. "For most of them, that's enough."

Garrick stared at him. "Why are you doing this?"

A deep sadness flashed through Brand's eyes, but he masked it quickly enough. He couldn't quite keep it from his voice though. "Because I do remember, and I never wanted it to come to this, but I had no choice." He bent his head. "I *have* no choice."

Garrick was confused. Did this mean Brand hadn't stopped being Garrick's best friend on his own? Was someone else behind it? "Sure you have, Brand," Garrick told him. "You just made one choice right now by telling me. You make your own life; you never let someone else rule it. So you have choices, you just have to make them."

"It's not that easy," Brand snapped, eyes flashing with pain. "You have no idea, Garrick, no idea!"

"That's right, I don't—because you suddenly stopped speaking to me!"

"I *had* to!" Brand yelled. He took a deep breath, calming himself down. "You don't know what it's like, because ultimately your parents let you do as you please. Mine never will!"

Garrick was starting to see it. Brand's father had always been a bastard, but Garrick hadn't known he was like that to his family. He was an arrogant, self-obsessed, power-hungry beast, and one reason Garrick's father did not want the leadership passed on. The main reason was simply that Garrick's father was power hungry and selfish, but it wasn't the only reason.

"You have to leave, Garrick. Take your witch and leave. They will do something drastic just to get rid of the witch, and it won't be good." Finished speaking, Brand turned on his heel, shifted in mid-step, and sprinted back into the forest.

Garrick stared after him for several moments, even when he was out of sight. He was realizing, now that it was too late, that something was not right with Brand. Hadn't been for a very long time. And he'd been too angry and bitter to notice.

But Garrick could do nothing for his old friend. All he could do was take care of Mihai, make sure he was all right. And according to Brand, if he drew this out any longer, Mihai wouldn't be.

He shifted and ran off, straight towards the direction of his cabin. He did not slow once, to intent on what was ahead. He had no breath left when he reached the cabin, but he jumped up the stairs before shifting. He threw the door open and stalked inside, taking in the empty front room. A sound came from the other room, and he jogged over.

Mihai was lying on the floor, his body twisting unnaturally. Low, pained groans escaped him. "Mihai!" Garrick fell to his knees next to him, lifting his head up so that it rested in Garrick's lap. Mihai's eyes opened, and Garrick drew in a sharp breath as he saw that they were completely black. "It hurts," Mihai whispered brokenly. "It hurts so much."

"It's your magic settling," Garrick told him. "You just have to wait it out. There's nothing to do. Not that I know off, at least." It was eerie how no white was showing in Mihai's eyes. But Garrick had never met a young witch before, all he had to go on was the old witch from Mihai's village, and her eyes had been difficult to see in the gnarled face. He didn't think he'd ever seen them properly, so he could not tell if they'd been normal eyes or black like Mihai's now were.

Mihai closed his eyes again as another flash of pain went through him. Worried, Garrick lifted him up and put him into bed. "I'll be right back, Mihai. I have something I have to take care off. You'll be alright." At least he hoped.

He dashed outside, where it was starting to darken. He brought his horse out from its small stable and saddled him. Then he rushed back inside and quickly stuffed the saddlebags. The two books for Mihai, what clothes he had lying around, the clothes the witch had brought for

Mihai and what food he could get into it. He grabbed three small books from his own bookshelf as well. He wanted to keep more, but knew the horse couldn't carry it. Not with what was already packed and Mihai on his back.

So he'd have to settle for those books, the clothes and food. He went to his secret stash of money and emptied it all into his pouch. They'd need all the money they could get—and why leave any of it? He wasn't coming back here again. When he left, it would be for good.

Garrick secured the saddlebags to the saddle before dashing inside again. Mihai was lying quietly now, eyes still closed and resting. "Is it over?" Mihai nodded, then opened his eyes to look at him. Garrick noticed in relief that they were normal again. He lifted Mihai up in his arms.

"What are you doing?" Mihai asked, startled.

"We have to leave," Garrick told him. "We have no time to lose." Grabbing Mihai's cloak from the hook by the door, he went outside and settled Mihai on the horse's back. He threw the cloak around him, fastening it good before untying the reins and giving them to Mihai.

"It's still light enough to see relatively well," Garrick said, looking up at the white, scared face. "Do you mind if I shift? I can better travel through the forest in wolf form."

Mihai shook his head jerkily. "Whatever is best for you," he whispered, gripping the reins tightly.

Garrick nodded gravely. "Then follow me." He wasted no time. Once he was shifted, he ran off into the forest, trying to keep to the well-worn path used by him for so many years now. He heard the clatter of hooves behind him and knew Mihai was right on his heel.

An angry, aggressive howl warned him that they were not the only ones running through the forest. Aware that they were now being followed, he listened more carefully to the sounds around them. Paws hitting dried leaves and fallen twigs. What were they trying to achieve, chasing them through the forest? They were already leaving!

A warg came leaping out of the trees at his right, hitting Garrick heavily in the side. Garrick stumbled, but quickly managed to regain his footing. Snarling, showing off his teeth, he turned to the other warg.

It was Brand's father. He really shouldn't have been surprised. The man was as aggressive as they came, so of course he was behind this.

They circled each other for half a round, then the other warg snarled and attacked. His jaws snapped after Garrick's neck, but he managed to twist around, barely avoiding the razor sharp teeth.

This wouldn't be like fighting with BrandGarrick never really used his teeth on him, and neither did Brand the few times he managed to win, but Brand's father was a completely different matter. He had no scruples.

"Garrick!" Mihai was shouting. Garrick looked around wildly, finally seeing him ahead. Mihai must have run past him at some point, most likely when Garrick had been pushed off course.

He was now surrounded by at least five wargs. They were slowly advancing on him, and even though his horse was used to wargs, Garrick saw that he was getting frightened. So was Mihai, his face was white in the low light. The sun was setting fast; it would be completely dark soon.

Garrick could do nothing for Mihai now. He wanted to, but he himself was under an attack from someone who would not hesitate to kill him. He was most likely disowned, and there was no chance of punishment should he be harmed. And he would, Garrick knew, because Brand's father had always disliked him, though Garrick never knew why.

He focused all his attention on Brand's father, hoping to get this over with quickly so he could get over to help Mihai. Mihai had nothing to save himself with. He was not battle-trained. He was just a young man who had lived in a village his whole life.

Brand's father was not letting him get the upper hand, instead Garrick was starting to worry he would actually win. It was getting harder and harder to avoid his advances. Garrick ducked one clawed paw, but another came towards him straight away and he was struck across the face. He fell heavily to the ground.

"Garrick!" Mihai screamed then, and Garrick jerked his head up. His horse was moving restlessly, but the wargs surrounding them seemed to hesitate, afraid of the hooves that could be deadly if they hit right.

Garrick looked at Mihai next. He was holding on tightly to the reins, his face still pale as a sheet. But his eyes... they were black as the darkest of nights.

All hell broke loose.

Garrick pressed himself further against the ground as the tree roots shot up high, slashing through the air and knocking everyone standing off their feet. Some of the roots knocked so hard the wargs were flying several feet through the air before meeting the ground rather painfully.

Mihai! Garrick dared lift his head and his eyes widened. Mihai was still sitting atop the stallion, eyes still black, but otherwise completely alright. The slashing roots weren't anywhere near him, but loose leaves were fluttering around the horse's legs, some even reaching Mihai's boots.

This is his doing, Garrick realised. *He's doing this!*

Mihai's eyes fell on him, and all was silent for a moment, then Mihai's eyes suddenly returned to normal. The leaves fell and the attacking tree roots were sucked back into the ground with a resounding *swoop*, leaving only silence.

Garrick stared at Mihai, and then glanced around. Every single warg was knocked down, most unconscious, but some of them just dazed.

Garrick jumped to his feet and trotted over to Mihai, who was whiter than ever. Shifting, he took Mihai's trembling fingers in his own. "You did good," he told the scared witch. "You saved us. Now, let's get away before they realise what's going on. Follow me." He shifted back to wolf form again and started for the path. They had no time to lose if they wanted to get far enough away before it got too dark to see anything.

It soon got too dark to continue. Garrick could've gone through the whole night, but neither Mihai nor the horse had Garrick's excellent night vision. Garrick shifted back to human form and went off to find some wood, leaving Mihai to tend to the horse.

When he came back, Mihai was sitting on the ground, back against a tree trunk and arms wrapped around himself. His head was bowed, so Garrick couldn't see his expression.

He quietly got the small fire going. He'd realised while gathering wood that he'd completely forgotten to bring a blanket. Garrick never had a need of one—if he should ever get cold, he could just shift. But Mihai was human, and so stuck with human limitations. If he were a trained witch it would've been different, but he wasn't.

What had happened earlier had not been under Mihai's control. It had been luck that neither one of them had been hurt. Mihai needed training and he needed it now. Thankfully the old witch had told him where to bring him. He didn't exactly know where it was, but he had a map and it shouldn't be too hard to find it once they got out of the forest.

"How are you?" Garrick went over to crouch down in front of Mihai.

"Afraid," Mihai mumbled. "I'm so afraid."

Garrick reached out hesitantly and slid his hand around the younger man's shoulder. It made him remember vividly that night Mihai had been stabbed and Garrick had kissed him in parting. The kiss had been brief, but it had given him a taste of his young witch—and he wanted more.

But too much had happened. Mihai was emotionally fragile, and Garrick did not want to put anything else on his young shoulders. He did not want Mihai to start to depend on him because he was the one being there for him. Yes, they were bonded, he was Mihai's familiar, but Mihai needed to be independent.

"It's all going to be alright," Garrick spoke in a low voice. "Eventually, it all will be. I promise."

"I have no family left," Mihai whispered. "They were never nice to me but at least they were my family. Now it turns out that they weren't. My mother is someone I have never met. Someone I will most likely never meet."

Garrick moved closer to him so that their sides were pressed together. "Sometimes we just have to choose our family," he replied softly. "I've never viewed my parents as my family. We've never seen eye to eye. I'm choosing my family, and I'm choosing you."

Mihai raised his head at that, staring up at him with wide eyes. They were so close now, Garrick could clearly see his irises. They were blue, a deep, clear blue. Very fitting for the thick, black wavy hair that fell around his face, softening the masculine angles.

Garrick slowly became aware of their hearts beating in synch. He could hear Mihai's heart just as well as his own, and it was almost as if he could feel it too.

Mihai dropped his gaze then and bent his head slightly, resting it against Garrick's shoulder. "Thank you," he whispered, "for everything you've done for me."

"You don't have to thank me," Garrick

answered.

"Yes, I do," Mihai whispered. "Because of me, you no longer have a home. You're not welcome in your own village."

"I've never really been welcome there," Garrick told him. "I've been thinking about leaving for a very long time. You helped me achieve that. So *I* have to thank *you*."

Mihai was silent, but Garrick somehow knew he was smiling.

"May I check your side?" Garrick questioned quietly. Mihai nodded at that and sat up properly, stripping off his cloak, belt and tunic. Garrick carefully removed the bandage and then blinked in surprise. The last time he'd looked at the wound, it had been red and raw — now it was nothing but a thin white scar.

"Has it been bothering you since we left my cabin earlier?" he questioned.

Mihai's eyes flickered in thought, then he slowly shook his head. "No, it hasn't."

This wasn't right. Even if Mihai's powers were at work, it couldn't possibly go this quickly. Garrick cast a wry glance at Mihai, the scene when they'd been attacked in the woods playing through his mind. Mihai had to be really powerful.

It made him a bit uneasy. The only witch he'd ever been in contact with was the old village witch, and she'd never shown any sign of her powers. But then, maybe she'd been too old.

Garrick had always wanted this, being bonded to a witch and experiencing something more than just staying hidden in the village. But with a witch of this much power – and untrained at that – Garrick felt some doubts.

Though, as he had no set knowledge, all witches could be this powerful... but not all of them were untrained. Witches were usually found young and trained until they had every aspect of their powers under control.

Garrick stood up and balled the bandage in his hands. There was no point in tying it back when Mihai's wound was completely healed. He stuffed it into one of his saddlebags, and went back to Mihai, who had lain down.

Mihai's eyes were closed, but Garrick could hear from his breathing that he was not yet asleep. It did not take long before his breathing evened out and Mihai was fast asleep, the day had had to take its toll on him.

Garrick shifted to wolf-form and carefully draped himself around Mihai. He was not going to be cold, that much Garrick was going to take care of.

Garrick opted for leaving the forest the next morning. Even if their destination lay at the very end of it southwestwards, they would travel faster on proper roads. And Mihai needed to sleep in a proper house, in a proper bed, not on the ground.

They travelled the whole day, only stopping for lunch and an early dinner. They reached a small village by nightfall and Garrick shifted back, walking besides Mihai and the horse until they found the inn. He went inside and paid for a room with a bronze and a few coppers from his pouch.

He only ordered the one room, but he could sleep on the floor while Mihai got the bed.

They ate supper at the inn as well, sitting at a small table for two in one corner. The horse was properly taken care of and put in the stable belonging to the inn. "What is this place we're going to?" Mihai asked, fiddling with the sleeve of his tunic.

"It's called Vortigern," Garrick replied. "Apparently it's some sort of castle, lying at the very end of the forest southwestwards."

"Why are we going there, exactly?"

"Because you need to be trained," Garrick told him, realising he had not told Mihai any of his plans. "The old witch spoke once to me of a powerful witch living there. Hopefully he'll be able to help us."

Mihai lifted his head, staring straight at him. "Us?"

"Yes, us. We're in this together. Have you forgotten the familiar bond? You will need extensive training in managing and using your magic, and a familiar needs to train as well for the bond to work properly."

"You know a lot about all this," Mihai commented.

"Not as much as I'd like," Garrick replied. "It's mostly stuff I've read in the few books I've been able to get my hands on. Some of it I got from the old witch, but when it came to familiars she wasn't very forthcoming. So that bond is what I know the least about. It shouldn't be like that. We're bonded and we should know what that means."

"We will." Mihai reached out and covered Garrick's hand with his own, squeezing gently. "If that witch is willing to help us, he will tell us what we need to know. If he isn't willing, we'll find someone else."

Garrick smiled softly, squeezing Mihai's hand back. "You're right," he chuckled. "We'll find out, or learn by ourselves. No matter what, it'll work out."

And in that moment, he felt confident that it would.

Garrick lay curled up on the floor, listening to Mihai tossing and turning in bed. An hour he'd been moving restlessly, not able to sleep, and Garrick knew he was still worried, even after their talk at supper. Shifting back, Garrick went over to the bed and sat down on the edge. "Mind if I join you?"

Mihai stilled. "No, not at all." He moved over slightly to give Garrick more room.

Garrick slid under the covers. They were warm and already smelled of Mihai, who was now lying completely still, seemingly afraid to breathe. "Have you heard the story of the princess that pricked herself on a thorn and fell into a deep sleep?" Garrick asked him softly, wanting to make him feel safe and forget about his worries for a while.

"No..." Mihai's voice was barely a whisper,

but Garrick's hearing was better than any human's and he caught it.

"Some say it's a true story, that the princess lived many ages ago. Others say it's just a made up story for children. I don't know what to think, except that it's a nice story." Garrick had never been told stories as a child from his parents, but Brand's mother was a great storyteller. When they were kids and had gone off to play in the forest, Brand had related the tales she'd told. Those had been great times, just lying in the forest, listening to fantastic tales of ages past.

Maybe that had sparked Garrick's own interest in what was outside the warg village, or maybe made it bigger, more compulsive. "The queen wanted her daughter to marry a prince and have children, but the princess was not interested in being tied to a prince, she wanted to be free, to make her own decisions." Garrick could slowly feel Mihai relaxing as he started relating the tale. "One day, when the queen and princess walked through the rose garden, the princess pricked herself on a thorn and fell asleep. No one could wake her up and the king and queen despaired. They tried everything, even bringing in the prince they wanted her to marry, to see if a True Love's kiss could wake her. But the princess did not wake."

Garrick turned over so that he lay facing Mihai in the dark. He could see him clear as day, though Mihai probably wasn't realizing that. "Then one day an exotic beauty arrived at the castle, and in desperation the king and queen let her in to see the princess, hoping she had some magic from the land she was from that could save their daughter."

"What happened?" Mihai asked curiously. "Did she manage to wake the princess?"

"She did. But not by any magic."

"Then what?"

Mihai's excitement to know the rest of the story made Garrick's skin tingle. And he couldn't help himself. He bent over and pressed his lips to Mihai's in a soft, chaste kiss. "With a True Love's kiss," he replied when he pulled back, his lips only inches from Mihai's.

Mihai's breath was shaky as he let it out, but he didn't seem displeased with the kiss. Not at all.

"And with the princess having found her true love, the queen relented on her having to marry the prince, and let her live happily ever after with her exotic beauty."

Mihai drew another shaky breath. "That was beautiful," he whispered.

"It certainly is my favourite," Garrick replied with a smile. "Will you be able to sleep now?"

"Yes. Thank you." So saying, Mihai curled into him, and Garrick could do nothing else but wrap his arms around him.

I'm falling in love with my witch, he thought. He'd never felt that emotion before, but it felt really good. So did Mihai, falling slowly asleep in his arms.

They travelled hard, keeping close to the forest, but out on the proper roads. Garrick had got many looks when they met people on the road, some afraid, some curious, some suspicious.

So apparently people weren't used to wargs here either. Garrick knew there were more wargs than those in his village out there, but he had never met an outsider and no one ever spoke of them. Maybe they too, just as his pack, lived secluded, away from humans. The looks he was getting sure supported that theory.

When they stopped for a break at midday, Mihai looked thoughtful. Garrick was curious, but didn't really want to prod, so he kept silent.

It didn't take long for Mihai to open up though. "I don't like travelling in open terrain," he commented softly from where he stood tying the horse's reins to a low hanging branch. Garrick had opted for resting close to the forest. "I think we should go back to traveling through the forest."

"Don't you want to sleep comfortably?" Garrick asked him.

"Of course I want that, but it wasn't so bad the night we slept in the forest either." Mihai patted the stallion gently on the neck, and the horse turned his head, his nose butting playfully against Mihai's shoulder. "People keep staring at us."

"At me," Garrick clarified dryly.

"No, it's not just you." Mihai finally turned around, coming over to sit next to Garrick. Garrick handed him a piece of dried meat, their meagre lunch for the day.

He had no idea how long this journey would take. The map he had was old and didn't have any concept of distance. They could be travelling for a few days, but could go on for a few weeks. He did not know just how big the forest was — it was already bigger than he'd ever imagined.

"They stare at me too," Mihai continued in a

low voice. "I think these... powers or magic or whatever it's called is doing something to me."

"Your eyes turn black when you use it," Garrick said. "They were completely black back in the forest when the pack attacked us."

"I didn't know that." Mihai touched under his eyes gently, as if he could feel for it. "Maybe that's why people stare. I think I'm using it without meaning to." He lowered his hands and cast a nervous glance Garrick's way. "Sometimes small rocks move off the road by themselves and leaves flutter off the ground, even when there's no wind."

Garrick stared at him for several moments. "I am not an expert on this, far from it. I really have no idea what's going on. But the old witch left you two books. She was very specific that you should have those two books. Maybe there's something in them?"

"She left me books?" Mihai looked completely taken aback. Then he bent his head and twisted his hands together. "We don't have time to read books; we should continue on. The quicker we get there, the better. I just want my life to go back to normal again."

"It will never go back to how it used to be," Garrick commented gently. "But once you get your powers under control, you can make a new normal for yourself."

Mihai smiled slightly at that. "Let's continue."

As Mihai had requested, Garrick ventured into the forest. It went slower, but Garrick had to agree—here there was no one to look at them funnily. It was just them and the forest, and Garrick loved the Forest of Fenris. It was his home, always had been. No one understood the forest quite like he did.

"Garrick, stop!" Mihai called, breaking Garrick out of his reverie.

Garrick slowly turned around, a bit baffled by the sudden stop, to see Mihai dismount and run over to a small bush. A bush with silver leaves.

Shifting back to human form, Garrick went over to grab the horse's reins. His nose caught a scent— "Mihai!" he shouted in warning, but it was too late. Mihai had already stepped on the nest, and three small slithering shapes came out hissing. "Mihai, get back on the horse!" Garrick held tight to the reins as the horse started moving worriedly.

Mihai stared at the worms, then he bent down and plucked several silver leaves off the Dragon tree. "We might need these," he called, holding the leaves up as if to show them off to Garrick.

But Garrick's eyes were not on Mihai or the leaves, because after the small worms came a big one, slithering slowly out of the hole in the ground. "Mihai!" he yelled in panic. "Get back here! It's a lindworm!"

That spiked a fear in Mihai, and he came running back, still clutching the leaves. His eyes looked around wildly as he clambered onto the horse again, looking for the deadly creature.

Garrick had just given the reins back when the stallion reared up on his hind legs, hooves kicking out in front of him. A low hiss from behind alerted Garrick and he turned, watching as the lindworm that, at first glance, looked very much like a big snake rose up on its front legs. The long, coiling head looked down at them and it was baring its razor-sharp teeth dangerously.

"Go," Garrick said, then realized Mihai couldn't hear him over the horse. "*Go!*" he yelled and hit the horse hard over the rump. The hooves hit the ground with a thump and the stallion shrieked in fright. Then he abruptly reared around the way they'd been going and set off. Garrick saw Mihai hold on tightly to the pummel, face white in fright.

Garrick took a deep breath, then shifted in mid-turn. Lindworms were deadly: if the poison didn't kill, the jaws would.

But as a wolf, he at least stood a better chance at winning. Looking up at the beast, a mix between a giant snake and a dragon, he felt fear settle. Back in the forest around where he'd grown up, lindworms were rare, especially ones as big as this one.

The reptilian eyes looked down at him, taking him in. Then it hissed loudly and dived, coming towards Garrick in a speed he couldn't match.

Garrick could only hope he'd get out of this alive.

chapter four
vortigern

Mihai held on tightly to the reins and crouched low atop the horse's back. He kept his head down so that he wouldn't be hit in the face by branches on the horse's wild ride through the forest.

He was afraid. He was afraid for himself, atop a frightened animal, going at high speeds through a forest with treacherous ground underneath. But he was mostly afraid for Garrick, who had stayed back there with the beast.

Lindworms... Mihai had never seen one before, but he'd heard of them. And nothing of what he'd heard was any good. Vicious, deadly creatures they were.

Garrick...

His fingers were getting tired from keeping

such a tight hold of the reins and his thighs were getting tired from keeping himself steady in the saddle.

A low hanging branch hit him across the head and Mihai crouched lower, burying his face against the neck of the horse. The mane whipped around his face, making it so he couldn't see anything, but at least he didn't have to be hit and hurt by the branches.

The only things he heard were the sounds of the hooves hitting against the ground, breaking twigs and dried leaves. He could hear nothing of Garrick or the lindworm.

He did not know how long the horse had been running, but it had to be a while. His arms and legs ached, and he felt himself sway the tiniest bit in the saddle. He let go of the reins with one hand to clutch at the pommel, desperately wanting to keep himself atop the horse.

He did not even want to think about what would happen if he were to fall.

The horse stopped abruptly, almost sending Mihai flying, only his grip on the pommel kept him from tumbling off. He sat up straight, looking around wildly. A wall, old, but safe and sturdy looking, was right ahead of him. Mihai lifted his gaze higher, catching sight of a tower against the sky – a fortress! It had to be the place they were travelling to.

Mihai turned in the saddle to look at the forest. It lay far back; the stallion had run awhile over the flat land before it dared to stop. Mihai desperately wanted to turn and ride back inside the forest, to look for Garrick. Garrick had done so much for him, he desperately wanted to do something for Garrick.

When he tried to turn the horse around, the mount promptly refused. Instead it completely disregarded Mihai's grip and hung its head, sucking wind and wheezing. Mihai pulled on the reins furiously, but there was no helping it. The stallion did not want to go back into the forest.

The fortress... there had to be people there!

As soon as the thought struck him, Mihai kicked the horse's sides, bringing the mount into a hesitant walk. Mihai kicked it again, harder, and the horse switched into a trot. He tried to urge it to go faster, but it refused, so Mihai settled for the trot. He did not like it, but it was obvious the horse could not gallop after the running it had done.

Now that they were in open terrain, the horse

let him lead and he turned it onto the road leading into the fortress. The gate was open and the hooves made a clopping sound against the paved road leading inside.

He could see no one on the way inside, but when he drew the horse to a halt outside the double doors leading into the fortress, the doors banged open and a person stepped out. He was impressive-looking, big and muscular with wavy blond hair and blue eyes. He wore a sword comfortably at his side, and there was no doubt in Mihai's mind that he knew how to use that sword.

"Help me," he called out, his voice trembling. "My friend... we were attacked inside the forest!" Mihai held onto the reins, panicked at the thought of getting down. He wasn't going to get out of the saddle until he knew that Garrick was safe...

"What attacked you?" The man came down the stairs. His voice was deep and masculine and carried well.

"L-lindworm," Mihai stuttered. "Garrick stayed back... I don't know what..." His voice broke off into a sob. He bent his head, not wanting this strange man to see him cry. "I could've helped him... I should've helped him..."

"How could you have helped him?" the man asked brusquely. "You don't even carry a knife. Lindworms are not to be taken lightly."

"Because he has magic."

Mihai whipped his head up and to the side at the masculine, yet melodious voice that came from the doors. Another man descended—this one was smaller than the other, lean and slender. He wore no weapons, only a long, flowing robe Mihai would've associated with women. This man wore it fantastically though. He had long, pitch dark hair and his eyes...

Mihai gasped. His eyes were completely black. Was this the way Mihai's eyes looked when he used his powers?

"I'll go look for his friend, Lor," the warrior spoke. "You take care of this one." And with that, the man was gone.

"I have to go with him," Mihai said frantically, looking around for the man, but he was nowhere to be seen.

"You will do no such thing," the witch said, because he had to be a witch. Those eyes were exactly as Garrick had described Mihai's eyes. "You are tired and scared and worried, and you will come inside with me."

That voice brooked no argument, and Mihai

slowly swung down off the horse.

"Leave the animal," the witch said as he turned to walk back up the stairs. "It will be tended to."

Mihai followed him slowly, flexing his hands tiredly. They hurt, but until he knew Garrick was fine, they would have to wait.

The witch led him into a small sitting room. There were five comfortable-looking chairs placed in the small quarters. Bookcases filled what was not taken up by a big window, the door and the fireplace. Mihai hadn't realized how cold he was until he was standing in front of the fireplace, feeling the warmth of it seep into him.

"Come sit down, little one. The warmth will reach you here as well." The witch motioned to a chair next to him, and Mihai nervously did as asked. Their chairs were turned slightly so that they faced each other, but Mihai looked at the fireplace. He didn't want to look into those pitch-black eyes.

They reminded him too much of what was happening with himself. And if Garrick... *Garrick*! Realization dawned on him and Mihai snapped his head up. They were bonded, meaning he could feel Garrick's heartbeat.

He closed his eyes and took a deep breath, trying to calm his own worrying enough that he could feel and hear anything but his own frantic heartbeat. Calm settled over him and his heart beat in rhythm, only to be joined with a second one. But this one was not calm, it beat fast, full of adrenaline. It told Mihai nothing other than that Garrick was still alive.

When he opened his eyes again, the witch's black ones were looking at him intensely. "Everything turns out for the better if you just sit down and feel it out," he spoke, as if he knew what had transpired. Perhaps he did know, he looked quite powerful. "Now," he folded his hands in his lap, eyes going to the fire. "I am Lorcan. The man you met outside is Tord. We live here at Fort Vortigern, just the two of us. What business do you and your friend have here? No one remembers Vortigern any longer."

"Someone remembered it," Mihai whispered. "The old witch back in my village … She told Garrick to take me here, that a powerful witch lives here. I need training."

"You are untrained."

It wasn't a question, but Mihai nodded anyway.

"How long have you known of your

powers?"

"About a fortnight, I think," Mihai murmured. "I didn't really have the powers, she said I was a potential. And then... she did something to me, something that killed her. And from then on I..." He couldn't continue. He didn't know what to say. He didn't know what to think about anything.

His life hadn't been perfect, with a family that despised him, but at least it had been calm... now it was all a jumbled mess. He felt like he was falling apart slowly at the seams. He felt he was keeping himself held together barely by not thinking about everything that had transpired.

Except now he was worrying himself into an early grave because of Garrick. Why hadn't he just run too? Why did he have to make sure Mihai got away, only to turn around and try to fight the beast? He should've just run...

But he was alive. Mihai had to stay content with that until he saw Garrick again. Hopefully this man — Tord — found him and brought him back to the fortress.

A commotion in the front hall brought Mihai out of his thoughts, and the witch — Lorcan — was out of his seat before Mihai could so much as blink. He threw the door open and stared at the sight that met him.

Mihai got up as well and stretched his neck, trying to look past the taller and wider witch. First he saw Tord, with a limp arm around his neck and Mihai felt cold. Then red hair came into sight and relief swept through him, because it couldn't possibly be Garrick...

Lorcan moved so that they could cross the doorway, and then Mihai saw it all. Garrick, alive and well, was supporting the red-haired man on one side, with Tord supporting him on the other.

A flash of a man with the same red hair shifting into wolf-form went through Mihai's head, and he took a step back in shock. This was the one that had attacked Garrick at his cabin. And who had attacked Mihai in the forest the first time he had ventured inside. He had seemed to hate Garrick.

So why was he here?

A knock on the door startled Mihai, and he turned around just as the door was opened hesitantly. "You still awake?" Garrick asked as he peered inside, seeing Mihai standing there staring at him. "Can I come inside?"

"Yes, of course." Mihai sank down on the edge of his bed and folded his hands in his lap. He hadn't seen Garrick since his return earlier. He had been too busy, together with Tord and Lorcan, tending to the red-haired man. Mihai had had nothing to contribute, so he'd left them to it.

Garrick closed the door after himself then joined Mihai on the bed. "Are you alright?"

"Yes, I am." Mihai looked at him. "Are you? You were worse off than me when we parted."

"I am fine." Garrick smiled sadly at that. "Before I could as much as attempt to fight off the lindworm, Brand was there. It happened so fast I'm not quite sure what even happened... but the lindworm retreated."

"I thought you two weren't friends?" Mihai questioned carefully.

"We were, many years ago," Garrick told him, "but then Brand just did a turnabout. I don't even know what happened. He just stopped speaking to me and started hanging out with those two goons, Evert and Joos."

"What changed?"

Garrick stared down at his hands for several moments. "Brand has been whipped. His back was... an awful sight. I think there's more to all of this than I've ever known. Before we left, Brand was the one to warn me what the pack was planning... I think the whipping was the price he had to pay for doing that."

Mihai did not know what to reply to that, so he kept silent, just put a reassuring hand on Garrick's forearm, hoping the gesture would be appreciated.

Apparently it was, because Garrick smiled softly at him, then covered Mihai's hand with his own. "Have you got any answers yet?"

"Not really, no." Mihai shook his head. "Lorcan and I didn't really get to talk much before you arrived with Brand. I've just been cooped up here, really. I didn't want to get in your way."

"You can never get in my way, Mihai," Garrick replied, voice low. His eyes were so intense Mihai had a hard time keeping his gaze.

Blushing, Mihai finally averted his eyes.

"It's late," Garrick said then. "And I see you're getting ready for bed. We shall talk more tomorrow."

Mihai raised his head, but did not know what to say. He wanted Garrick to stay, he didn't mind his company at all ... but he did not know how to express himself. He had never been good at that, and had never had the need.

"Good night, Mihai." Garrick's hand slid around Mihai's neck, caressing him gently, then he pressed a kiss to his forehead.

Mihai gazed after him as he left the room, still feeling the press of Garrick's lips against his forehead. He almost felt... giddy.

Mihai had just got dressed and was trying to get some control of his hair the next morning when there was a knock on his door. Before he could even turn around, Lorcan swept into the room.

"Good, you're ready."

"Ready for what?" Mihai turned, fingers still toying with his curls.

But Lorcan didn't answer, just looked him up and down. "Come with me." At that, he turned and was out of the room.

Mihai hurried after, not asking more questions seeing as he apparently wasn't going to get any answers. Lorcan moved gracefully, even though he was still wearing a gown. Today it was silvery black and sparkled when the light from the windows hit it.

The light grew dimmer as they walked through the fortress and Mihai realized they were moving down into the dungeon. Soon there were no more windows and their path was only lit by torches hanging on the wall, each a good distance from its neighbours.

Lorcan took a fast turn, entering a room whose closed door had been hidden in the dark. Mihai quickly followed, finding the confining, eerie darkness of the dungeon somewhat scary. He did not want to stay down here alone, that was for sure.

"This is my work-room. I want you to have a look at this." Lorcan stood in front of a wide table and Mihai moved to stand across from him. On the table lay several objects, trinkets and things that could only really be considered garbage.

"What is this?" he asked, confused.

"Just look at these." Lorcan made a wide movement with his hand, indicating everything that lay on the table. "Does any draw you in more than the others? Do you feel a certain want or need or *pull* towards any of these things?"

Mihai blinked, then looked down. A white feather lay closest to him, but he felt nothing for it. Next there was a cup of water and again he did not feel what Lorcan seemed to want him to feel. He felt nothing for the burned, charred wood either. But then... a small pile of dirt lay closest to Lorcan, and it seemed to pull Mihai in.

No! Mihai shook his head, knowing his eyes were going to change and fighting it. He did not want this. He did not know what it entailed. He did not want another episode like the one when they'd been attacked by Garrick's pack. It had been necessary, else Garrick and he never would've got away, but he still didn't want a repeat.

"Stop fighting it," Lorcan snapped. "Let it come to you. Let it flow through you naturally. There is nothing wrong about this."

But Mihai didn't want to. And he kept fighting it.

"What are you afraid of?" Lorcan asked. "What scares you?"

"Everything," Mihai replied, voice low and strained. "I am afraid of these powers that I suddenly have that I know nothing about. I am afraid of what I can do with them. I have already done a few things I wish I hadn't. I am also afraid that these feelings I have for Garrick, and him for me, are because of our bond, of my powers."

"You really know *nothing,* do you?" Lorcan stared at him in wonder. "Come here." He went over and sat down in an armchair standing in one corner of the room, motioning Mihai to take the other.

Mihai sunk down hesitantly, not knowing what to expect.

"Garrick is your familiar because his magic blends with yours," Lorcan explained.

"Garrick doesn't have any magic," Mihai interrupted quietly.

"Isn't it magic that makes him shift from human to wolf form? All those that have that ability are called wargs—and yes, they're a race apart from normal humans. But it *is* magic. He might not even know it himself, but it is true. That bond that you two share, it can't make feelings happen just like that. Magic can't force feelings. So if you feel something for your wolf, and he feels something for you, it is not because of your magic bond, but because you have, as happens to everyone, fallen for each other."

It was good, getting to know more about a bonding, but Mihai's ears right now were all for the latter part.

"A witch's familiar can be a friend, a lover, even an enemy. The bond doesn't care about the feelings between the two parties," Lorcan continued. "All it cares about is that the magic is compatible. A familiar can even be family, your brother or your sister or even a parent, and then it would be quite impossible for romantic feelings between the two parts, wouldn't it?" Lorcan turned his head to smile at him. His eyes were still as black as the darkest night.

Mihai nodded, averting his gaze. "But what is the meaning of the bond? I mean, I can feel Garrick, I know he's alive. But besides being able to feel his heartbeat right next to my own, I don't see the purpose of being bonded."

"Because your magic levels each other out. If you get out of control, Garrick can take that, because your magic can't hurt him. A familiar is not affected by his witch's powers, no matter how powerful that witch is. So a familiar can thus calm his or her witch's powers down if they do get out of control without fear of any harm."

"So that's the purpose of the bond?"

"It's the gist of it," Lorcan replied. "There are all kinds of loopholes, different from one bond to the other. It's experimentation, being bonded. So you just have to figure it out as you go along."

Lorcan stood up with a grin and went back over to the table. "Now that your fears have been laid to rest, are you ready to try this again?

A witch is what you are, and it's nothing to be afraid of. It's a gift, not a curse."

Mihai went over to stand opposite him again and he took a deep breath, trying his best to let his fears go. His eyes landed on the pile of dirt. It drew him, it called to him... Taking another deep breath, he let his restraints finally go, hoping he wouldn't regret doing it later.

And as the pile starting thinning, spreading out in all different directions on the table, Mihai knew his eyes were now a mirror image of the witch across from him. He lifted his head slowly and met the eyes of the man across him, only now they were completely normal. The irises had a hazelnut brown colour to them, and they seemed to sparkle with mirth.

"You're an earthwitch," Lorcan spoke. "And a wild one at that."

"What does that mean?" Mihai questioned. "Earthwitch? Wild?"

"A wild witch is a term for witches who are not bound by the limitations of incantations and chants. You can control your powers with your mind and your power is immense in wild form. A so-called normal witch can never stand up to you, because they have no chants or spells or incantations to mimic the extent of what the mind can do."

Lorcan leaned forward and his eyes turned black again. He looked down at the table and as Mihai followed his gaze, he saw the dirt slide over to gather in a pile right in front of Lorcan's hand.

"I was raised in the capitol, being bound by what the crown decides is best," Lorcan explained. "When I found out about what could really be done... it took me years to move past the restrictions of what I had learned. But you... you don't have to travel the hard way. You have immense power lying at your feet right from the beginning. I'm going to train you. Not only do I have an affinity for earth, but for the other elements as well and you can never find a better teacher than me."

Mihai stared at him, taking in everything Lorcan was telling him. If he was going to resign himself to this course, he might as well learn everything that he could.

"And as for being an earthwitch..." Lorcan stopped to think. "Regular witches can do spell casting, no matter what element. It's the incantation that counts. But I have found that once one gets past all the words, into what the scholar's call wild, you are limited to one thing and one thing only. For you it's earth. You can use the earth like no one can, because it is your core element. You can bend it, you can use it, you can create it... you are the earth and the earth is you."

Mihai nodded mutely, mind whirling with what Lorcan had told him thus far.

"If you'd been found when young, you would've been moulded into a regular witch, and you could've broken out of it like I did. But now... You're too old to learn the basics of witchcraft. It won't take. You only have one choice and that is to learn the power given to you and learn it well. I am quite good at what I do, and though I have never had an apprentice, I would be willing to take one as talented as you. Are you willing to let me teach you, Mihai?"

Mihai swallowed nervously. This would change his whole life... but it was already changed. He had to learn, else he would end up hurting not just himself with his powers but others as well. And Lorcan seemed like a good man, and in complete control of his powers. Who better to teach him?

Mihai slowly nodded his head, placing his future in Lorcan's hands.

Mihai liked to spend his free time in the forest, just walking through it, smelling it and feeling it. The Forest of Fenris did not scare him anymore; instead it had become a place of peaceful rest.

Sometimes Garrick joined him for his trips, but today Garrick was busy training with Tord. They'd started spending their days together when Mihai had been cooped up with Lorcan, and Garrick had become quite skilled with a sword. He hadn't been before, relying more on his wolf-form than anything else. Now he was gaining muscles and becoming quite the warrior.

Mihai found he liked it. Not that he hadn't liked Garrick before, but just as Mihai he was growing as well. Despite Mihai's initial hesitancy, they were both growing for the better.

Mihai reached out to a low-hanging branch and let it twine around his hand using just a tiny portion of the magic Lorcan had helped him get under control. He still had much left to do before he could go off on his own, but he had learned much for the short time he'd been at the fort.

Mihai pushed away other low-hanging branches and soon found himself in a small clearing. A big rock was half-way burrowed into the grass in the clearing and atop it sat a man half-way turned away from Mihai. A man with flaming red hair ... and flames playing across his palm.

Mihai's gasp alerted the man to his presence, and Brand turned sharply, eyes instantly finding and cutting into Mihai. The flame instantly vanquished and he curled his hand into a fist atop his thigh.

"You're a witch?" Mihai asked, dazed as he walked into the clearing.

Brand roughly turned his head away, not answering.

"I won't tell anyone," Mihai offered weakly.

"Like that matters," Brand replied. "That witch, Lorcan, seems to know. At least he's looking at me when he thinks I'm not watching. But I'm not like you — I don't need training."

"But if you've had none... if you're a wild — "

"I've taught myself through the years," Brand snapped. "I've had no other choice. I'm good at it. I don't need someone to tell me what to do; it's not like I'm showing off to anyone."

Mihai saw it then. He saw Brand's anger and bitterness for what it was. He saw beyond the mask Brand confronted the world with. Brand wasn't bad. He wasn't sweet either but Mihai couldn't blame him for turning out like he had —

Mihai could've just as well turned out like him. Brand was keeping a wall between himself and everyone else, not letting anyone in.

"Garrick was your friend once," Mihai told him quietly. "He wouldn't mind being so again."

Brand jerked at that, then winced in pain. It had only been a few days--his wounds couldn't possibly be healed, so Mihai could understand how even such a small gesture could hurt his wounded back.

"Yes, he would," Brand snapped in reply as he got to his feet. "He knows nothing about what happened back then and I can't tell him."

"Why not?" Mihai pressed. "He'd understand..."

Brand's hard, green eyes met Mihai's. "Yes, he would." Then he strode off further into the forest.

Mihai looked after him. Brand might've tried to kill him... but he'd warned Garrick about the pack's plans and had been whipped and exiled for it. He had good qualities. They were just burrowed deep within under the anger and the bitterness and under whatever had transpired back in his childhood with Garrick.

"Were you just talking to Brand?"

Mihai whirled around at the quiet voice behind him and found himself facing Garrick. "Yes, I kind of interrupted him here. It wasn't much appreciated."

Garrick smiled slightly as he stepped closer, standing so close that Mihai could feel his body-heat. "How are you doing? You've been so busy these last couple of days I've hardly seen you."

"Right back at you," Mihai replied, smiling sheepishly. "But I'm doing fine. I'm learning to control my powers. Lorcan says that's the most important thing now, that the theory and basics can come later."

"I have to agree with that," Garrick said, "because the power you showed in the forest close to my village... it was immense."

Mihai grew serious at that. "I don't want that to happen again. It was not a good feeling, it was quite frightening. If I have to go to that extreme again, I want to have it under control, so that I know I won't actually kill anyone. Or hurt you."

Garrick's hands came up to cup Mihai's face, turning it up so that Mihai had no choice but to look him in the eyes. "You're getting the training you need, just as we hoped for. Everything will be fine now." He bent down and pressed his lips to Mihai's.

This kiss was not at all like the first kiss Garrick had given him, when he'd been laying hurt in Flynn's house. That had been firm and quick and playful—this was soft and gentle and loving. And this time Mihai responded to it.

Mihai hesitantly slid his arms around Garrick's waist, but when Garrick only drew him in closer, Mihai grabbed a hold of the back of his shirt, sighing into the kiss. It was turning harder, more passionate, by the second. Everything else, every sound of the forest, was blocked out. He only focused on Garrick. Garrick's lips against his, Garrick's arms around him, Garrick's front pressed against Mihai's own.

He hadn't known Garrick for very long, but he had utterly fallen in love with him. He had never felt like this when he'd thought himself infatuated with Flynn, which told him how different this was. How much *better* this was.

Mihai sighed as Garrick drew back, and his cheeks flushed with color from both happiness and embarrassment. He stared hard at Garrick's neck, not quite ready to meet his eyes again.

"We're bonded, and always will be," Garrick whispered. "But even if we hadn't been... I would never leave you. You have me spellbound, my lovely little witch."

Mihai laughed softly at that, then bent forward slightly, resting his head against Garrick's collarbone. "I was afraid my feelings were just because of the bond, but I know better now. The bond doesn't control our feelings, only we do. And I wouldn't want to leave you either, even if I could."

Garrick chuckled and wrapped him up in a tight hug.

Mihai couldn't help the spark of magic going through him then, which caused the fallen leaves to flutter around them. He let go of Garrick's shirt with one hand and held it out, palm down. When he focused, and from the top of the dried leaves and twigs, a bright white flower erupted.

Garrick stepped back as he caught sight of it. He stared for a long moment, then looked back at Mihai. "We might not have the lives we used to," Mihai spoke up quietly. "And I think, for both of us, that that is for the better. Now we can make our own life, eventually find our own home and purpose. And I'm looking forward to that."

"So am I." Garrick grinned reassuringly, then he moved forward again and caught Mihai's lips in another kiss. Mihai relaxed into it, finally letting his joy and happiness out as he embraced Garrick's wide shoulders. No, he was not living the life he used to, and he would never go back to it. What he had, here and now, was all he needed. All he would ever need. And when his training was up, they'd figure out what to do next.

Together.

the
hunt
ress

about the story

When you're looking for your own destiny—it finds you.

Liv runs away from her spoilt and priviliged life as a princess to find her own destiny in the world. She knows she's made out for something other than prancing around in pretty dresses.

On her journey she meets a woman like no one she's ever met before—and by journeying with her, Liv finally discovers her own place in the world, like she's been longing to find out for so long.

chapter one
the huntress

The inn was crowded, the noise level close to unbearable.

Liv was sitting in her dark corner, enjoying the simple life of peasants. Men drank and boasted amongst each other, women sat in groups of four or five and whispered and giggled. They were all dressed in simple clothing that Liv never would have worn in the castle.

Since she'd left her privileged life, however, she'd acquired proper wear for a commoner's life. It was a bit coarse, and it itched, but she could not go around wearing her fancy dresses out in public anymore. Here she did not want to be the princess — she did not *ever* want to be the princess again. Here no one knew her, and if they had ever seen her, they would not recognise her dressed as she was now.

Liv took another spoonful of stew, eyes not stopping their roaming.

The inn was driven by a fierce-looking woman no one seemed to want to provoke even the tiniest bit. Two girls worked the floor, slipping from one table to the next, delivering food or ale and taking empty mugs and plates with them back to the kitchen.

This was nothing like what Liv was used to at the castle—and she was fascinated by it. She was not meant to live a princess' privileged life; she was meant to live amongst commoners, live a normal, hard-working life. Not that she was working, she was travelling through the country, but if the opportunity presented itself... she might take it.

Liv had only stopped at the inn for some hot supper, and when she was done, she would be on her way. She camped out in the open at night, even if she could afford to rent a room; she preferred sleeping under the stars. Her parents and siblings back home would be appalled if they knew, but Liv cared very little about what they would feel. It was a bit uncomfortable, and a bit cold, but the sight of the stars made up for it aplenty.

The only thing nagging her was leaving Bas, which gnawed on her conscience. She could have perhaps talked him into coming with her, but on the other side... Bas had known about the marriage her parents planned to force her into and had not told her about it. *"When you're a princess, you do not get to decide over your life,"* he had snapped. *"Duty to family and country comes first, no matter what. It is time for you to learn that, Liv."* And so saying he had stomped out of her rooms in anger.

So Liv did not feel as bad as she normally would have felt. He had had it coming, the stupid cat. Her familiar or not, sometimes she just had to be on her own. She could not count on Bas for everything — he was not her lover. He was her bonded yes, but he was so holier-than-though that sometimes Liv wanted to smack him upside the head.

He was older than her and he was her tutor but that did not give him the right to think he was so much better than her. He had been like that for as long as Liv could remember and she was sick of it. So it was good to get away from him too, though she could not stay away forever. He was her familiar, after all, and she did care for him. He was more of a brother to her than her real brothers were.

She just had to make her own life before she went back. She had to find her place in the world, because it was *not* being a princess and living in the castle all her life, marrying a noble and giving him children. She would be miserable then, she knew it.

That was why she was here. To find her own destiny.

The inn fell silent around her, bringing Liv out of her deep reflections. Looking up, she scanned the crowd. Her eyes landed on a woman entering the inn. Everyone was staring at her. She did not look like anyone Liv had ever met — peasant or noble. Her hair was blue-black and braided into at least a hundred thin braids that she kept away from her face by a sash she had bound around her head. As she stepped further into the room, Liv noticed that it was not just the colour that was unfamiliar — tiny beads were braided into it, as were coloured feathers and silk.

She wore a white linen shirt, quite common for peasants, with a black-leather vest laced over the top. A heavy wool cloak fell over her shoulders, thrown back now as she entered the inn, and a sword hung comfortably at her hip.

She was tall, taller than Liv, and slender, but it was also obvious by that sinewy body that she was all muscle.

This woman was not a normal commoner. No one Liv had ever met held a candle to the exotic beauty. No woman Liv had ever met would dress herself in breeches like that. The custom for women was skirts, though Liv had to admit that she liked what she saw. She let her eyes travel up and down the woman again as she moved through the room towards the counter.

She was too far away for Liv to hear her voice, but she spoke to the innkeeper and soon seated herself at the last available table in the room. She took off her cloak and threw it across the other chair, and then she leant back and let her eyes roam the room.

Liv could not muster the strength to look away, until those eyes—silver eyes—met hers, she turned away in embarrassment. She felt her cheeks blush and took another spoonful of stew to try to get her thoughts over to something else. She soon found her eyes going back to the black-haired woman, however, watching as she was given her own bowl of stew by one of the maids.

Liv wondered what the woman did for a

living. She certainly was not a farmer. That much Liv could tell. The way she carried a sword told Liv the woman was used to its weight there, and she was most likely excellent at using it. Which pointed at a violent way of living.

Liv finished the rest of her stew as she glanced out the window. The sun was slowly sinking, and she had to get moving if she was to find a good place to camp before nightfall.

She put some money on the table and started reaching for her cloak, only to freeze as a scream pierced through the loud noise of the inn. Everything quieted and Liv could swear she could have heard a pin fall in the sudden silence.

The scream came again and now people started moving. Liv did too. Forgoing her cloak, she made for the door, pushing her way through the tall men standing in front of her.

A woman was running towards them, terrified by something Liv could not see.

Liv walked down the steps to meet her, and the young female practically fell into her arms. "What is the matter?" Liv asked worriedly. "Are you hurt?"

"L-lindworm," the woman gasped out and turned her head to stare with wide, terrified eyes at something behind her.

Liv lifted her head, following the woman's gaze. Now she saw it. Something came towards them, slithering on the ground and making hissing noises. Frowning, Liv held the trembling woman closer.

"I was just inside the forest, getting water... and suddenly there it was: A nest of small lindworms. I tried to leave them to themselves, but then the mother came..."

"Shh!" Liv stroked the woman's hair, eyes trained on what looked like an enormous snake coming towards them in quick speed. It did not seem to mind the rough terrain.

"Get inside!" someone shouted behind her, but Liv found she could not move. A lindworm... She had read about them, but never seen one in real life. It really did look like an enormous snake, but the illustrations in the books had not been nearly as terrifying as a real-life worm.

The lindworm reared up, jaw opening wide in a snarl. The woman in Liv's arms screamed in terror, fighting free of Liv's embrace, and then stumbled past her, clattering up the steps to the inn.

Liv stood up slowly, staring at the monster

closing in on her. Now it looked more like the illustrations. Still a lot like a snake, but now she could see an equal resemblance to the dragons it was said to be distantly related to. The razor-sharp teeth took up three rows in its mouth, and the fangs were three times as long as the rest. The scales gleamed dark green and black spines went from its forehead all the way down its back to the end of its pointed tail. Spikes also came from atop its nostrils, and bigger ones more resembling horns erupted from above its ears.

A lindworm only had front legs, with big, razor-sharp claws. Having no hind legs did not seem to bother it as it rose up into the air, balancing on its tail.

Liv stared up at it, trying to figure out a spell that would work against this creature. Her mind came up blank. Lindworms were no threat in the capital, and so no one had ever mentioned a spell that could defeat one. Liv drew a shaky breath, then took a step back, debating whether to stand perfectly still or run. The lindworm's eyes were on her; it could see her and it was going to attack any second.

It threw its head back on another loud hiss, before it dove towards Liv, who was frozen in place. *I'm going to die*, she thought in a panic. *I'm going to die because I don't know how to defend myself against this creature!*

She could see the white in the lindworm's eyes, and then her vision was suddenly blocked by hundreds of tiny braids flying through the air as the woman they belonged to drew her sword and slashed it through the air.

Liv watched in astonished wonder as the sword cut straight through the lindworm's neck, severing its head from the body. It wailed loudly once before the head finally fell to the ground, closely followed by the rest of the body, which completely splattering Liv in its blood.

"Here you go."

Liv gratefully took the cloth that was held out to her. She ran it over her face, getting the worst off the blood off, but she knew some still stuck to her skin. Not to mention her hair and clothes.

"I'll go ask the innkeeper for a room and a bath," the same voice spoke again. "We're going to get you cleaned up."

Liv looked up in time to watch the exotic woman's back disappear up the stairs and into the inn. *She's going to help me get cleaned up?* she thought, dazed. Bending her head, she stared at her clothes. They were ruined, that much was obvious. She would never get the blood out of them. They were her only proper peasant clothes and now she had to purchase new ones.

"Come on."

Liv gasped in surprise as her arm was grabbed and she was dragged towards the inn. Once the surprise faded though she went quietly with the strange woman, hoping the bath would be ready. She smelled horrible and wanted nothing more than to get out of her ruined clothing.

"They are going to bring the bath right up," the woman told her as she pushed Liv into a small room containing a bed, a nightstand, a small wardrobe and a table with two chairs. "Do you have anything else to wear?" She looked Liv up and down, face unreadable.

"In my saddlebags," Liv replied. "They might not be of common stock, but they ought to do until I can purchase new ones." Amala looked at her at that so Liv hurried to tell her the rest. "I left the saddlebags in the stable with my horse. She is a chestnut mare. And I left my cloak at a table downstairs."

"I'll get it for you. You just hold tight and

wait for the bath." So saying, she was gone.

Liv did not have time to dwell on the mysterious woman, as the innkeeper herself and a very big, muscular man came up with the bath, accompanied by two of her maidens, both carrying buckets with hot water. One had a cloth and a towel tucked under her arm as well.

"Here you go, miss," the woman said gruffly as the two maidens emptied the buckets into the already half-full bath. "You get cleaned up quickly. Lindworms are nasty stuff."

Liv thanked them heartily, and then wasted no time stripping out of her clothes as they left the room. She slipped down into the warm water and sighed in pleasure. Her skin, though it smelled like it, had not received a splatter of blood, but her hair was still full of it.

She scrubbed her body with the soap the maid had brought with her until she was sure the smell was gone. Once her body was clean, it was time to do her hair, and she could not do that while still staying in the water. The bathtub was too small and tight for her to be able to dip her head into it while sitting, so she stood up and reached for the towel left on the table.

The door opened and the black-haired woman entered, carrying Liv's saddlebags over one shoulder and holding Liv's cloak in the other. She stopped, one hand still on the handle of the door, as she caught sight of Liv.

Liv felt the warmth spread up her neck and cheeks, and she quickly grabbed the towel and wrapped it around herself, turning her back on the other woman in embarrassment. Opting for ignoring her at the moment, Liv knelt next to the bath and bent over, pushing her long, blonde hair down into the water. She used the soap on her hair as well, scrubbing away at it. The blood tinged the clear water a light red.

"It's dangerous facing a lindworm, like you just did," the woman told her curtly as she moved into the room, closing the door after herself. "If I hadn't been there, it would've killed you and no one else would've lifted a finger. Lindworms scare people here; they are their greatest fear."

"I can defend myself," Liv replied, somewhat snappishly. "I have just never seen one of those creatures before and it baffled me."

"You haven't seen a lindworm?" It sounded almost like an offense that Liv had not. "You are obviously not from around here then if you've never seen one. Where are you from?"

"The capital," Liv replied. She grabbed the

cloth and used it to dry her hair. "Born and raised."

"A city girl." The woman rested with one hip against the table, arms crossed underneath her breasts. "And what's a city girl doing so close to the Black Mountains?"

"Travelling." Liv stood, trying to use her fingers to comb through the tangle of her hair, with no apparent success.

"With no weapons, no escort?" The woman raised one dark eyebrow. "I find it hard to believe that a young woman like yourself would put herself in such danger. If it's not lindworms you have to look out for, it's robbers and bandits. A lindworm would be kinder, trust me."

"Contrary to what you seem to believe," Liv replied tartly, "I am perfectly capable of taking care of myself. I am a witch, just graduated from the University." That was a small lie, she had not actually graduated yet, but this woman did not need to know that. "Yes, the lindworm had me paralysed, but that will not be the case next time. I do not want to experience that again, thank you very much."

Liv went over to her saddlebags and rummaged in them for her comb. The other woman was standing entirely too close for comfort. As soon as she had the comb she went over to sit on the bed. Guilt for snapping at the woman tore at her, and she sighed softly. "Thank you for saving me," she told her, voice low, but carrying in the small room. "I really appreciate it." She swallowed, not quite sure if she was using the right words.

"This is what I do. I save people and villages from lindworms," the woman replied. "They are nasty creatures, destroying not just crops but the herds as well. The most usual way of dying around here is by a lindworm attack. Or a bite. It has a deadly poison in its fangs."

Liv struggled with her hair as she listened to the woman talk. It was all so strange. In the capital it was not animals they had to worry about. The usual way of dying back home was of age or sickness, or from the after-effects of a fight, if one obtained a knife wound or a head injury.

"Move over."

Liv startled to find the woman suddenly standing beside her, but she did as ordered. The comb was taken out of her hand and her hair brushed back over her shoulder to hang heavily down her back. Liv dared barely breathe as the woman started combing through her hair.

"I'm Amala," the woman said then, voice soft. "Huntress of lindworms and protector of the small villages in and around the Black Mountains."

"I am Liv," Liv introduced herself. "Just a witch."

"There's nothing wrong with that," Amala replied. "As I've heard, witches can be quite powerful."

"We are." Liv closed her eyes and bent her head slightly back, enjoying having someone other than herself doing her hair for a change. "If you know the right spells and the correct incantations."

"And that is something you all are required to learn by heart? The spells and the incantations?"

"It is hard to learn them all," Liv chuckled, her mood improving vastly now that she was clean and having her hair combed. "We learn the most basic, but the more complicated spells we keep written down. Most witches always carry a book containing spells with them. It is the most important thing a witch owns. Nothing can ever replace it if it is lost." Liv kept her own safely secured in her saddlebags, spelled so that only she could touch it and open it.

"There. Your hair is done." Amala handed her comb back, then stood up from the bed. "It was nice meeting you, Liv, but it's getting dark and I better be on my way."

"What?" Liv turned around, surprised at the sudden talk of leaving.

"Don't worry," Amala smiled briefly. "I paid for the room tonight. You relax and get on your way in the morning."

"But..." Liv searched for words, but couldn't come up with something intelligent to say. "Let me come with you!"

Amala turned around, regarding her curiously. "You were stalled by one lindworm. Why would you want to come with someone like me, who hunts them?"

Yes, why do I want to go with her? Liv asked herself drily, but she already knew the answer. "Because I think what you do for people — common, defenceless people — is good and noble. I want to be a part of it. I know defensive and offensive spells. I shan't freeze like that again, I swear to it."

Amala still looked reluctant.

"Just give me a chance. If I do slow you down, or mess up, I will gladly go on my way."

Liv held the towel closed as she turned around to face Amala completely. "I just want to do something that matters and this does. You help people. You make them feel safe. I want to be a part of that too."

Amala tilted her head up, staring up at the ceiling for a long moment. She sighed and looked back down at Liv. "Alright, you can come with me. It would be nice to have company for a change. But you should still sleep here tonight."

Liv frowned. "What about you?"

"Don't worry about me." Amala made for the door. "Sleep well, Liv. We leave at dawn." She closed the door after her, leaving Liv to her solitude.

Liv sighed and lay down on the bed. *What have I got myself into now?* she thought, playing with a lock of her hair. She did not regret it though. She wanted this. Wanted to be a part of something good, something that helped people, and this was it. Nothing was going to stop her.

Liv watched the mountain range looming ahead in wonder. The mountains were the tallest she had ever seen, and the entire mountain range was covered in forest, except for the peaks.

Not even two days into her time spent journeying with Amala, they had reached her destination: the Black Mountains. Only the mountain range shielded the land from dangerous territories. Not a lot was known of the land beyond the mountains, but it was said to be a great wasteland where people rode dragons and breathed fire just like the marvellous beasts themselves.

Of course, all of that was just hearsay. It sounded too incredulous to be true, but those were the stories. Liv could not argue with them.

"There's a small village further up the mountain that is continuously plagued by lindworms," Amala told to her. "It has been three months since I was there last. Let us hope it is still standing."

Liv had not yet seen another lindworm and she felt her stomach churning at the thought that she soon would. At every stop they had made the past two days, she had been continuously going through her book, trying to learn both defensive and offensive spells that she thought would help against the reptilian creatures.

They were closing in on the mountains fast. The Black Mountains loomed high into the sky, the angle of the sun causing them to cast the land in front of them into shadow.

Amala urged her horse into a faster gallop and Liv followed. Liv had always snuck off for a ride whenever she had free time, but she had certainly travelled slower when she had been on her own. Even still, she was glad she was used to riding, because Amala was relentless with the speed.

Not that she was complaining. She liked that they were on their way to actually help people from a very real danger. She was with a beautiful woman, whose company she enjoyed more every day.

Amala was like no one Liv had ever met before. Not just because of her exotic look, but because she did not treat Liv any better than others — they were on common ground. She was not a peasant and Liv was not the princess. They were equals, and that was something Liv had never felt before.

Back home everyone was so formal, so phony with their friendliness, wanting to get closer to the princess. Out here she was liked for the person she was, not because of her higher status. No one here knew who she really was and she preferred to keep it that way.

She did not like the lie, but she did not regard herself as a princess now. She was a witch, first and foremost, and she was helping Amala on her mission to keep people safe. Why did anyone need to know she was a princess? They would regard her differently. They would not be able to trust her as their equal. It was better to keep quiet about it. Even to Amala, no matter how much it bothered her.

The day was slowly turning into evening, darkness seeping over the landscape. It made their road even darker as they had reached the mountain shadows and were riding into the little village a bit up the mountainside. The village lay on a flat expanse, trees cleared back around it, yet still surrounding the village all the same.

"See why this village attracts the lindworms?" Amala nodded to the trees as they let their horses walk slowly up the road and into the village. "Surrounded by forest on all sides. Lindworms thrive in the woods, especially when there's people and food right in the middle of it."

"But they seem to be all right," Liv offered, looking out over the quiet houses. "Nothing is broken. All looks calm."

"I have taught them a manner of protecting themselves," Amala replied. "They do not carry swords here, but I taught them to use what they have. Knives and pitchforks, mostly. But it can be enough if you're swift and strong."

Liv glanced over at her. "Maybe you could teach me some of that fighting? I might be a witch, but being able to physically defend myself would be nice."

"Sure, I can do that. Even have an extra sword." Amala patted her saddle gently, but the sword she was talking about was wrapped in a blanket and strapped to the back of the saddle. "Now, this village actually has an inn. It only has three rooms, but they don't have many visitors here, so nothing else can be expected. We'll have somewhere to stay and food to eat. The woman living there makes marvellous stew."

Liv smiled at that, her stomach rumbling in agreement. Chuckling, she stopped her horse when Amala did and jumped down.

"Hi, there!" A man came towards them, greeting Amala warmly. "Let me get your horses settled, ladies. You two go in and my wife will have food on the table for you."

"Thank you, Tob. That is greatly

appreciated." Amala grabbed her saddlebags and slung them over one shoulder, then made for the inn.

Liv grabbed her own saddlebags as well and hurried after her. The inn was small, only one story tall, but it was nice and homey and the fire in the front room was lit. Liv felt instantly at ease.

"Lady Amala!" A very small, very round woman appeared in front of them, beaming up at Amala as she dried her hands on a cloth. "I knew you'd be back soon. I have some food boiling on the oven. Are you hungry?" Her eyes slid over to Liv and her smile grew a fraction. "You've brought someone with you this time? Hi, my lady, I am Elly."

"Pleased to meet you," Liv replied with a smile and small curtsy. "I am Liv."

"Come on, ladies, sit down. I'll bring some food out for you in just a moment." She ushered both Amala and Liv over to the table closest to the fire, then bustled back into what Liv could only assume was the kitchen.

"They seem nice," Liv told Amala, sitting down with a sigh in the comfortable chair.

"They are." Amala issued a small, wry smile. "This is my favourite village." She then turned sharp eyes on Liv. "When we get up in the morning, we're going into the woods and I will teach you some swordsmanship, as per your request."

Liv felt her stomach knot nervously at that. "That is much appreciated," she said and she meant it. "I really do want to learn, though I expect I will be horrible."

"Who isn't their first time?" Amala grinned. "You'll do great, Liv. I am an excellent swordswoman, and I believe you'll take to it quickly."

Liv could only hope so, though she doubted it. She was normally slow at learning. It took relentless studying and training for her to pick things up. She would do her best though. That was all she could do.

Wood clashed against wood as Liv parried Amala's strike. She tried to hold the stick in position, but Amala was much stronger than her. She easily pushed Liv's hands out of position and held the tip of her own stick to Liv's throat.

Liv stepped back, and instantly collapsed on the ground, letting the sword roll out of her hand onto the grass. "This is exhausting," she groaned. "I am not made for this." She had never held a sword in her life—and if she had known just how heavy they were, she never would have agreed to it.

"Don't women in the capital get warrior training?" Amala sat down next to her, crossing her feet under herself.

"A woman can choose it at the University, but few do. I did not—I had enough to do taking my magic courses. They might not be hard for the body, but they certainly are hard for the mind."

"Why don't more women take the warrior path?" Amala questioned.

Liv shrugged, though it was awkward, as she was lying flat on the ground. "It is just looked down upon. Women are weaker than men physically, so men should be the fighters, women the nurturers. That is the way it is among the royalty and the concept has spread to the rest of the people. I can say for certain that no noble woman has chosen to fight, at least not in my time. Those that do choose to fight are commoners—people who do not have much else going for them."

"That's bollocks." Amala tilted her head back to look up at the sky. They were in a small clearing in the forest that Amala had found the previous day. "Men might be stronger than women physically, but women have other attributes. Like, we're smaller, faster and more flexible. A woman can get close to an enemy and have him out of commission by using those skills instead of facing the opponent straight on."

Liv tilted her head to the side, looking up at Amala. Her profile contrasted against the trees behind her. Even overcast, the sky shone light on her, making the blue highlights in her hair all the more visible. The braids were still tied back by the sash she used as a headband. Liv found the braids to be quite fascinating. She had never seen anyone with quite that colour of hair and certainly not someone with that many braids. It had to take a full day to braid it all.

She turned her head away when a rustling sound reached her ears. The ground started shaking slightly and Liv propped up on her elbows, frowning. "What is that?"

Amala slowly got to her feet, sword gripped tightly in one hand as she let her eyes travel over the woods around them. Liv stood up as well, snatching up her own sword, though she would not be much help with it if something were to happen.

The rustling was coming closer and the shaking grew in size. Liv stared at the ground and saw the leaves at her feet move with the ground's quaking. "Amala?" she asked, her voice full of dread.

Amala stood poised to fight, eyes trained straight ahead.

Something burst out of the tree line ahead of them, something enormous and grey and ugly. Liv screamed.

"Troll!" Amala shouted, grabbing ahold of her arm. "Run!"

chapter two
the troll

"Run, Liv!" Amala shouted at her. "I cannot fight a troll and win!"

But Liv could not move. Not because she was paralysed with fear this time but because she felt magic. Powerful magic nearby. And it certainly could not be the ugly, hairy troll approaching at high speed having such powers, so someone else had to be out and about in woods...

Suddenly, tree roots shot out of the ground and wrapped around the troll's ankles and arms, stopping it quite effectively and keeping it locked in place. The troll, big ugly brute that it was, howled in anger and thrashed about but the tree roots did not budge.

Liv watched, completely mesmerised. She could feel Amala pressed up against her arm, watching as well. The troll was completely stuck and not happy about it, as indicated by its furious roaring.

An arrow came from behind Liv. It moved with such speed that she did not even see its flight before it pierced the troll's chest. The troll instantly stopped struggling and turned to stone. It cracked apart, each huge piece of stone falling to the ground with loud crashes.

Liv whirled around, hoping to see the one that had killed the troll.

"What the—" Amala mumbled next to her.

Two people stood a distance away, just past the tree-line. The one furthest back had dark brown hair that curled around his neck and over his ears, with a fringe that covered almost the entirety of his brow. The other one, the one in front, still held a bow in his hands. He had black hair that fell around his face in soft curls and his eyes... his eyes were completely black.

"Who are you?" Amala demanded as she stepped forward in front of Liv. "Who are you that you can kill a troll?"

"You should not be out in the woods by yourselves," the one with the bow and the black eyes spoke. "These are dangerous territories."

"And I keep the villagers residing here safe," Amala snapped. "So don't tell me what danger is. I know it well enough."

The other man stepped up to his companion's side. This one's eyes were strange as well, the pupils were black, but instead of the iris and the white of normal human eyes, his were an odd mix of yellow and orange. Not human eyes, that was for sure.

She could not read them. Though the set to the man's jaw could have been agitation or annoyance, she could not quite decide which.

"Then keep safe," the second one spoke up, his voice deeper than the first. "And keep out of way of trolls." The two seemed to simply vanish into the woods. They were out of sight as quickly as they had arrived.

Liv let out a shaky breath, her eyes straying to the cluster of stone. "Was that really...?"

"A troll, yeah." Amala turned to the stones as well. "Quite an adventure for you. Your first lindworm, then your first troll. Lindworms aren't unusual here, but... a troll. That is strange indeed." Her eyes swept the woods.

"Why is that strange?" Right then, Liv felt every bit the sheltered princess that she was.

"Trolls usually keep to their territories, which lie in the Jotun Mountains," Amala explained, "and we are very far from those mountains."

"But surely they must want to wander?" Liv questioned, feeling silly, but the pile of rocks had her twitching in nervousness. It was unsettling, that whole scene. She did not like it. "Creatures are curious by nature."

Amala cast her a look before going back to watching their surroundings. "Trolls are to the Jotuns what Neanderthals once were to the humans."

Liv blinked, not quite understanding.

"Trolls are big, ugly, primeval brutes, stupid as the rocks they become when killed," Amala explained. "Speaking of killing, I have never seen anyone actually kill a troll."

"What?" Liv stared at her, frightened. She remembered what Amala had shouted when the troll had arrived, that she could not fight it and win.

"The only way to kill a troll, that I know of, is to bring it into direct sunlight." Amala's hand twitched closer to the hilt of her sword. "It kills them the exact same way as this one was killed, by turning them into stone. But piercing a troll with an arrow... a troll's skin is almost as hard as a dragon's scales. It is impossible to penetrate. But this man, he managed it. I wonder how."

Liv bit her lip. She had nothing to offer — she

was just as confused as Amala. Even more so since Liv had never experienced anything outside the capital before. Yet here she was, on her own, with a warrior woman for a companion meeting lindworms and trolls. She had chosen this path herself, so she was in no position to complain. It was still overwhelming. And yes, frightening, but having Amala there felt safe, even if the woman had admitted to not being able to kill a troll.

"Let's go back to the village," Amala told her, turning away from her perusal of the woods. "It's starting to darken. We've been away long enough. If trolls are so far out of their territory, there could be more dangers out there. Trolls scare lindworms because lindworms can't kill trolls and the worms know it."

Liv shivered at that and obediently followed Amala back the way they'd come.

Liv sat cross-legged on the floor, the contents of her saddlebag covering the floor around her. She grabbed her pouch, the one that she could tie to her side. Her grimoire was too big for it, it had to stay in the saddlebags, but she gathered all her herbs, taking extra care with the one Dragon's

Treasure leaf she had left.

The Dragon Tree was extremely rare and the leaves highly valued. Only a witch could harvest the leaves, thus their name, but once they were plucked anyone could use them. They were highly powerful if used properly and extremely dangerous if used otherwise.

Liv glanced up at Amala, who was sitting cross-legged on the bed, her sword lying across her thighs. Amala was running her hand almost lovingly over the hilt, which Liv now noticed was made of what could only be gold and bedecked with tiny diamonds.

"That is a beautiful sword," she said, successfully drawing Amala's bright eyes to herself.

"Yes, it is," Amala replied, her hand moving to grip the hilt tightly before letting it go again. "It's been in my family for generations."

Liv saw an opportunity to get to know more about this exotic companion of hers and she instantly took it. "Do you see your family often?"

Amala's hand tightened on the hilt again and she bent her head to look at it. "No, I do not."

"Because you travel so much?" Liv could not stop herself from pursuing the subject.

"No, because they do not approve of me," Amala replied tersely.

Liv frowned at that. "How can they not approve of you? They are your family." She might not like her family but she still loved. Some of them, anyway.

"Because I did something I should not have done," Amala told her, voice cold. "So I was banished from my tribe, never to return again. All I had were the clothes I wore and this sword."

Liv eyed the sword again. It had to be a very expensive, very valuable sword. "They let you leave with it?" she asked incredulously.

Amala raised her head, meeting Liv's gaze right on. "Once a sword has been passed on, it can't be taken back," she replied stonily. "This sword's been mine for so long it's become a part of me. Taking it from me would be worse than death—and it's something that is never done in my tribe." She turned slightly, putting her sword away. She was obviously done with the conversation.

Liv's mind was running wild. Tribe... that likely meant Amala was not from Lore. Could she be from either the Dragon or the Jotun Territories? Or maybe from across the ocean?

But then again, some did refer to themselves as tribes in Lore as well. Shifters, for example, could refer to themselves as a tribe. At least, that was what she had been taught, by Bas.

Bas... Liv wondered what he was doing now. She knew he was alive, though he was not close enough for her to feel his heart beat any longer. She guessed such a distance could weaken the perks of the bond. She did not mind particularly, except it was strange... she had always felt Bas' heartbeat and it was weird that she now did not. She had never heard of not being able to hear it, even from such a distance, but then she had never had any interest in researching it.

She missed Bas, she did. At the same time it was good being away from him. Being bonded to someone like Bas who was so unlike herself... it was not easy. She knew Bas resented it sometimes, when they were at their worst.

Liv sometimes wished she could share such a close bond with someone that she had more in common with. Someone she liked, someone who would be more than a friend...

Her eyes slid to Amala, taking in the fit body that looked so good in those tight clothes, the hundreds of tiny, black braids falling down her back, those brilliant silver eyes not like any Liv had ever seen.

"We're leaving tomorrow," Amala announced, startling Liv. She averted her gaze, focusing on getting her spare clothes folded and back into her saddlebags.

"We are not staying here anymore? What if there is an attack?"

"There hasn't been one up to now. We can't stay here any longer." Amala turned back to face her, but Liv kept her head bowed. "We'll travel through the woods, looking for worms. If they won't come to us, we go to them."

Liv could hardly argue. Amala was the experienced one here — Liv was just tagging along. If Amala said they would leave, that is what they would do.

"What did you make of those two men we met earlier, those who killed the troll?"

Liv had been thinking about one in particular — the one with the black eyes. He had made the tree roots do what they had done. She was certain of it. He had shot the arrow that pierced the troll's skin.

"I don't know." Amala rode a little ahead of Liv, eyes perusing the woods on each side of the small road they travelled on. "They were an odd pair. The first one showed power like I've never seen before, being able to kill a troll with just an arrow. The other makes more sense, at least. I believe he was a shifter. A wolf shifter, going by those eyes of his."

"I noticed his eyes. I have never seen a real wolf before, and certainly not a wolf's eyes."

Amala cast a look back at her. "You are a sheltered young lady, aren't you?"

"Well, yes," Liv agreed. "I have never been far outside the capital before."

"So this is your big adventure?"

"It is an adventure, all right, and it is quite big."

"What do you plan to do when the adventure is over?" Amala questioned. "When you grow tired of it, or just feel done with it all?"

Yes, Liv, what do you plan to do then? "I do not know," she admitted. "All I know is that I cannot go home and go back to the life I had. I cannot marry just for the sake of marriage and spend the rest of my life producing babies."

Amala snorted in amusement at that. "Isn't that what we women are supposed to be for?"

"You have made another life for yourself," Liv pointed out. "You seem to be liking it just fine."

"That's true." Amala turned serious again. "Not every woman is cut out for marriage and bairns. Especially not if you don't find the opposite sex attractive. That counts for men as well."

Liv stared at Amala's back. Had she just admitted to not liking men, but women? Or had it just been in general, because as she had said, there were many that did not find their opposite gender attractive. It was completely normal, but as nobles... If you wanted your line to move on, a woman had to bear the child of a man.

Liv was not worried about continuing the line. She had sisters and brothers for that. All she wanted was to be happy—and she knew she could not be happy with a man. At least she had never found any of them attractive before. Not even Bas, and Bas was a very striking man.

Amala was a striking woman, with her sharp, brilliant eyes and long, braided hair. Not to speak of her skill with the sword and her fine body showing perfectly in tight clothes.

Shaking her head, Liv shoved those thoughts away and focused her attention on her surroundings. The sound of running water reached her ears and Liv urged her horse a bit faster, knowing that the mare was as thirsty as she was.

The road came to a bend and when she rounded it, she saw a bridge. Underneath it ran a river, only a few feet wide and it looked shallow enough to wade across with water that was so bright and clear she could see the bottom.

Both she and her horse were eager as they passed Amala, trotting down the slope to get to the river. Liv jumped down off the mare's back and let the horse lower her head to drink.

At her side, Amala appeared with her own horse. "Do you want to take a break?"

"Can we?" Liv looked at her hopefully. They had been riding all day through the stifling forest and all she wanted was to lay down in the shade and relax for a bit.

"We're not in a hurry." Amala smiled slightly. "We're just looking for lindworms. Maybe one will come to us while we rest." She let her horse stay at the water's edge and went back to the slope to lie down.

Liv followed her lead, lying down on the grass with a sigh. "We should sleep here tonight," she muttered, staring up at the treetops. They swayed gently in the wind, the leaves rustling, almost covering the perfectly blue sky overhead. "This is nice."

Amala did not reply, and Liv found herself dozing off. The grass against her back, the light breeze playing with her hair and over her face, dulling the heat of the summer day, the sound of the river, of the horses when they moved, the sound of Amala's breathing next to her... it all lulled her into a peaceful doze.

Tremors brought her back awake, and she blinked in confusion. Was she trembling? But no. It did not come from her, it came from the ground.

"Liv, get up," Amala spoke carefully from beside her.

Liv shook her head, trying to get rid of the sleepiness. The ground still moved beneath her and Liv looked up at Amala in confusion. Amala's head turned first to one side, then the other, eyes going back and forth.

"You need to run, Liv," Amala told her, voice low.

"What is it?" Liv pushed herself up on her knees.

"A troll!" It came as a shout as the huge beast appeared upriver.

The horses jerked up at her scream and noticed the troll immediately. Liv's mare instantly bolted into the river. Amala's horse stood back for a moment, then took off after the mare.

"The horses!" Liv shouted. She got her feet beneath her and started running down to the river where they had crossed.

"No, Liv, not the river!"

Amala came after her and grabbed her hand, roughly turning her around and shoving her towards the grassy slope she had just been sleeping on. Liv tripped in her skirts and fell, landing hard on the grass. She crawled her way up, breath erratic from fear. When she got to the top, she got a hold of the woodwork of the bridge and hauled herself to her feet. When she dared a look down, Amala was coming up the slope behind her. The ugly brute of a troll came running down the river, the water splashing around its hairy feet. This one was more brown in colour than grey, as the other had been, and even more hairy.

"Run across the bridge!" Amala yelled at her. "Now, Liv!"

Run across it? Liv stared at the troll rapidly approaching. It would hit the bridge right on, and it was not making any sign of slowing down.

"Now, Liv!" Amala yelled again. "Come on, you'll make it! I'm right behind you!"

Liv stopped thinking and just ran, her boots thudding against the wood of the bridge. She could hear the heavy breathing of the troll now. She knew it was closing in, but she did not realize just how close it was until she heard a scream and the cracking of wood behind her.

Liv fell to the path on the other side, and quickly turned around to see what was happening. The troll had indeed crashed into the bridge, breaking it completely, and Amala... she had fallen into the shallow river beneath. She was obviously hurt, as evidenced by how she struggled to get to her feet.

Liv turned her head, watching in fright as the troll turned around. It started forward again, sniffing the air loudly as the small, black eyes searched the ground. It spotted Amala.

No! Liv scrambled up, eyes wide as she saw that Amala still could not get to her feet. The water was coloured red around her, and it seemed to Liv from where she stood that Amala was favouring her left leg.

The troll let out a roar, terrifying Liv like nothing else. *It is the blood*, she thought, panicked. *It can smell her blood – and it does not like it! Or it likes it too much...* Either way it was approaching Amala, who was in no condition to defend herself.

Liv's mind raced. She had to help Amala, but what could she do? Amala was the strong one, the one she had been counting on since they had met.

What was it Amala had said, about killing a troll? The only way for a troll to die... was from direct sunlight!

Liv did not think, she reacted. She yelled the incantation for the only spell she could think of, holding her hand out towards the troll. When the last word of the incantation left her lips, her palm lit up and rays of bright light went in every direction.

The troll did not even have time to notice what was happening before it promptly turned into stone. Liv fisted her hand, effectively breaking the spell. A few moments went by in complete silence before the stones shattered, falling into the shallow river, water splashing.

"Amala!" Liv ran down the slope, all but falling flat on her face. Amala was still lying in the river, struggling to get up.

Liv waded out, not caring that she had soaked her boots and skirt. She grabbed a hold of Amala's arm, hauling her up to her feet. "Are you hurt?" Liv had to ask, though it was obvious she was.

"My thigh." Amala held one hand over her left thigh, and now Liv could see blood pouring out from beneath her fingers. She draped Amala's other arm over Liv's shoulders, giving her support. "A piece of splintered wood cut me up. Pretty deep too. It hurts like a—" She groaned in pain as she tried to take a few steps.

"Let's get you on land," Liv stressed, worried. "We do not want you to bleed out in the water. If you lean on me, can you make it?"

Amala nodded. "I can take pain, Liv. I am not a useless damsel."

Liv smiled slightly at that. "I know you are not. Now come on, I need to check on that wound."

They got to dry land all right, though Amala's jaw was clenched tight, her expression stony. Amala lay down gently on the ground, her hand still pressed against her wound.

"I need to cut up my breeches."

Liv crouched down beside her and, with some difficulty, ripped her breeches up around her wound. It was a deep gash on Amala's thigh, obviously created by something sharp like a piece of wood from the ruined bridge as Amala had said.

"You need to figure out if you know any spell that can hurt or kill a lindworm," Amala told her suddenly, her startlingly silver eyes meeting Liv's. "Fresh blood attracts them and if there's anyone nearby now we're in trouble. I can't stand on my foot right now, so I can't wield my sword."

Liv heard the warning loud and clear. Swallowing heavily, she looked down, back at Amala's wound. "I know basic offensive spells, but the bigger ones... like the one I used on the troll, are written in my book. Which is in my saddlebag, which is who knows where by now. It was pure luck that I managed to kill it." Liv sighed. "I am not actually a witch... I have not graduated. I left before graduation. And if you want to be a proper witch you cannot quit after graduation either, you have to choose a specific field to go into..."

"And have you? Chosen a field?"

"I... I don't know." Liv shook her head.

"You were about to graduate before you left," Amala pointed out. "You must've had some idea what field you wanted to get into."

Liv stared hard at her hands. She had been

through a number of fields in her head. The field of teaching, of showing young ones how to master their powers. The field of study, of figuring out new ways to use magic. What had really drawn her the most was the field of healing. Liv had always been good at healing, much more so than offensive spells. She did not want to cause anyone harm, though of course she would do it if it was a life or death situation, like it had been with the troll. Amala's life...

Liv closed her eyes. She had been able to heal Jorek once when they were little, when he had gone and fallen down the big oak tree in the garden. He had been bleeding profusely and Liv had managed to not only stop the blood, but heal the tear in his upper arm as well. There had not even been a scar. Of course, they had kept that a secret, because Jorek was not allowed up in the tree to begin with.

"Could you bind the wound?" Amala's voice broke into her thoughts. "There's nothing else for it. It'll hurt for a while, but it'll start healing. We'll just have to move slower."

"No!" Liv exclaimed, startled. She could not, and would not, let Amala walk around hurt, not when there was a tiny possibility that Liv could help. "Lay still. Do not talk. I'm trying to concentrate." She put her hands over Amala's wound, holding them there gently. The blood was starting to slow. It would begin clotting soon. Liv closed her eyes again, bringing up those long-ago memories of healing her brother, of that time her horse stepped wrong in the woods outside the city...

She felt the power surge through her, going down her arms to settle in the palm of her hands.

"Liv," Amala groaned then, not in pain this time but in wonder, causing Liv to open her eyes. Her head was tilted up and she saw the treetops swaying gently against the clear, blue sky. She could not say how she knew that the wound was healed, but she did know, and she took her hands away. Blood still coated them, and Amala's trousers, but where the wound should have been there were only smooth skin.

Amala propped herself up on her elbows, staring first from Liv, down to her thigh and back to Liv again. "What did you just do?"

"I healed you," Liv replied faintly.

"Is that a common skill for witches?" Amala was frowning.

Liv licked her lips, and slowly shook her head. "I have healing abilities. I have not used them since I was a child and have never told anyone. I think... I think maybe it is what I want to do. Heal people, that is. You do so well with being the strong warrior protecting everyone from lindworms." Liv met Amala's stare. "I want to be there, by your side, but instead of doing the killing of the monsters, I want to heal those that have been hurt. I..." She swallowed heavily. "I think this is what I want to do. No, I know it is. Healing you now, it felt good, and not just because you are you, but because for once I mattered. I did not freeze up in fear. I actually did something good. And it makes *me* feel good." A sudden calm settled over her as she said it, and she knew it was true. Being a healer, that was her calling. That was her destiny.

Amala continued to stare at her for long moments, then she sat up further and bent towards Liv... and Amala kissed her. Liv gasped, startled, but when it clicked in her brain that Amala actually *was* kissing her, she was quick to kiss back. Liv grasped Amala's shoulders, holding onto her tightly. Amala was now perfectly fine, but for the first time, Liv realised just how scared she had been for this woman that she barely knew. She knew Amala enough to know that she wanted to keep on kissing her, for Amala to continue kissing Liv. Right now, that was all that mattered.

A creaking sound broke them apart. How long they had been kissing, Liv could not say. It felt like they had been kissing for hours and yet for no time at all.

"I got blood on you," Liv said then, dazed, as she saw that Amala's shirt was smeared with the blood that had coated Liv's hands. "I'm sorry."

"Liv..." Amala's eyes were locked on something behind her. Liv slowly turned around, dreading what she would see. There was no lindworm, no new troll. What she saw was the splintered wood of the bridge suddenly shooting up from where it had fallen and growing back together. Before she had a chance to blink, the bridge was rebuilt, looking exactly as it had before the troll had crashed into it. Except now it had been repaired.

The two strange men from their first meeting with a troll were crossing it. Both Liv and Amala got to their feet as the two men descended the slope. Liv stared hard at the strangest of the two, the one with the black eyes. Only they were not completely black now. They were the eyes of a normal human being.

"How did you ladies manage to defeat a troll?" The one Amala said was a shifter asked, his strange eyes flickering to the heap of stones. "There is no direct sunlight in the woods."

"I am a witch," Liv told him in a low voice. "I did a light spell and it calcified the troll immediately."

The black-haired one, the one with the now normal eyes, nodded approvingly. "Good work. Are you making it your purpose to get into it with trolls then?"

"We are just passing through," Amala replied. "We aren't looking for trolls. It seems, however, that they might be looking for us."

The black-haired one smiled slightly at that, but his partner's focus was not on them any longer. He turned his head to the road up the slope, watching it steadily for a few seconds. "It seems that more than trolls are out looking for you two," he said then, his canine eyes flashing in the sunlight coming through the tree branches. "They have your horses."

"That is our cue." The other one started walking upriver, but stopped and turned to look back. "We make our permanent residence at Vortigern. If you ever find yourselves in need... you are welcome there."

Liv started at that, but the two were already walking away at quite a speed.

"That has any meaning to you?" Amala cast her a wry look.

"Yes," Liv whispered, "Vortigern... long ago, the University lay there until it burned down. They did not build it up again, for reasons unknown, and instead moved it to the capital. There are stories. Always there are stories."

Amala looked like she wanted to ask, but the sound of hooves brought her attention to the road. "Let's get up there. I don't want to meet whoever it is all the way down here."

Liv nodded mutely, following Amala up the slope. She came up behind her so that Amala shielded the road from her, and Liv hesitated for a moment before stepping to the side, worried about what she would see.

When she saw, she wished she had never moved.

chapter three
the end

"Liv!"

The voice whipped out, terse and angry, and Liv flinched back before regaining her composure. Taking a deep breath, telling herself she was not afraid, she straightened her back and met her brother's hard gaze.

"What are you doing here, Jorek?" She cast a wry glance Amala's way, perfectly aware that she had never told the woman who she was. The cat would be out of the bag soon, so to speak. Jorek was not going to keep quiet now that he was here.

With him he had Bas. Bas sat atop his black stallion, face set in stone and eyes locked on Jorek. Liv put a hand over her heart, still not able to hear Bas' heart beating in sync.

"You're shutting me out?" she asked him

incredulously.

Bas' eyes slowly turned to lock on her. "You left." His tone was neutral, but Liv knew he was being condescending. "One thing happens that you do not like and you leave."

"I cannot let them decide my life for me," Liv argued. "I have a right to have my own say."

"No, Liv, you do not. Sometimes you just do not have a say in the matter. Not when you are a princess of the realm, and certainly not when you are a lowly shifter bonded to her." Bas abruptly turned his head away and Liv realised he had not meant to let the last part slip.

What had Bas been forced to give up for her? She could not remember a time when Bas had not been there. What had he been, where had he been, before he had got stuck with a young princess with witch potential?

Amala moved restlessly next to her and Liv turned to her. Amala's expression was closed, eyes hard as they locked on Liv's.

"Amala, I—"

"You just neglected to tell me that you're a princess?" Amala asked, voice low and terse.

"I just... It does not matter," Liv replied meekly.

"Of course it matters," Amala snapped. "If

I'd known you were a princess, I never would've brought you."

"Now that is unfair," Liv accused. "Just because I am a princess I cannot experience the life you live? Simply because I have noble blood? I am no different than anyone, noble or peasant. I am me, and I want to live my own life." She stared hard at Amala, trying to make her understand. "Amala... I never meant to deceive you. If I was open about whom I was, no one would treat me like an equal. I just want to be someone's equal." She bowed her head, swallowing hard.

"Of course they wouldn't," Amala said coldly. "No one treats royalty like equals."

Liv's temper flared again and she looked back up at Amala. "You really are no one to talk, Amala. You are doing the exact same thing. I do not even know who you are. Yes, I know you were banished from your tribe, but what tribe is that? Are you even from Lore? Shifters live in tribes, but you do not have a shifter's eyes. So tell me, Amala, just who are you?"

When Amala did not answer, just stared at her, Liv turned to Bas. "Give me my horse. Now."

He gave the reins over without a word and

Liv took them angrily. She patted her mare's nose softly, staring into one big eye. The horse was the only one here that was not currently angry at her.

"I do not care what you are up to out here in nowhere land," Jorek spoke up. "You are coming home with us. Now."

Liv stared up at him. "I will go home with you, Brother. But only to tell Mother and Father that I am renouncing my title."

Jorek whipped his head around to stare at her. "You will not—"

"I will!" Liv shouted. "I will not live a life of luxury, being manipulated by cunning nobles and forced into a marriage of convenience. You might be happy living that way, as our other siblings are, but I will not!"

"It is part of being royalty," Jorek argued. "You do not have a choice."

"As I said, I will renounce my title," Liv told him stubbornly. "That is my right. When I do, no one will have any say over my life. I can do what I want."

"You will be poor," Jorek pointed out. "You are a spoiled little twat, Liv. You really think you would be happy being poor? You cannot wear your fancy dresses, boss servants around, or expect to get your way all the time. You will have to fight to get food on the table every day. It will exhaust you and then you will be begging to come home."

"How do you know how peasants live?" Liv asked him, voice rising with her temper. "I have been living like a peasant for some time now and I am not complaining. I have been happier this short while than I have ever been."

"You really want to be poor?" Jorek asked incredulously.

"I think that commoners, who have to work for what they want and need, are happier and more appreciative than those who do not." Liv firmly believed that, after witnessing these people since she had been on her own.

People in the villages she had visited were happy and content and knew how to have fun — real fun, without any motives behind it. It appealed to Liv, much more than court life. She hated living at the castle, surrounded by the cruel manipulations of the nobles.

"If you feel that way, Sister, then you will come home with us and tell our parents yourself," Jorek snapped.

Liv gripped the reins tighter at the thought of facing her parents. She did not want to, but she knew she had to. If anything she owed it to them to be honest, to tell them herself. After running off like she had... she had to go home, show them she was fine, and tell them of her plans.

"I'm leaving." Amala's voice broke Liv out of her reverie. Liv did not have a chance to turn to look at her before Amala rode past, having got her horse back and mounted it without Liv even noticing.

"Wha—" Liv blinked, confused for a moment before she realized that Amala was leaving. "Amala, wait!" She mounted her own mare, a little clumsily in her hurry, and hurried after Amala, reaching up to her right before the bend in the road.

"What do you want from me, Liv?" Amala asked her. "You just agreed to go home, so our adventure is over. I'm on my own again, I get it."

"No." Liv quickly shook her head. "I do not want you to go on alone. I want to go with you. But I owe this to my parents." She stared into Amala's silver eyes, silently begging the woman to understand. "But I do not want to leave you, so I would like it if you would come with me."

Amala's eyes were hard, cold. An astonished expression fleeted across her face at Liv's last sentence before she schooled herself. "You want me to go with you to the capital?"

"Yes." Liv stressed the word, hoping Amala would understand just how important this was to her.

"Why in the name of all the gods would you want that?" Amala demanded. "I do not belong in a city. And your parents—the King and Queen—will certainly not approve of me as your..." She stopped for several seconds, hesitating. "...your companion," she concluded meekly.

"But you are not just my companion." Liv steered her mare closer to Amala's horse, so that their feet were touching. The kiss they had shared, it had been like nothing Liv had ever felt. She had never felt good when being kissed, the few times someone had dared, but when Amala had kissed her, the world had tilted on its axis.

Amala stared at her, face unreadable. Liv was not to be deterred by anything, not now that she was finally going to prove a point. So she reached out, wrapped her arm around Amala's neck, tangled her fingers in some of the tiny braids, and drew Amala towards her. Liv bent closer as well and their lips met softly, neither of them moving for several moments.

Liv closed her eyes, hoping Amala would reciprocate, because Liv had taken the first plunge. Now it was Amala's turn.

She took it, reaching out to grab a hold of Liv's waist, drawing her body as close as possible when on horseback as she started kissing Liv for real. Liv sighed into it, opening her mouth and welcoming Amala's warmth.

She did not know how long they kissed, just as their first time it seemed to go on both endlessly and in the span of a moment. All she knew was that Amala's eyes had warmed and a small smile tilted one side of her lips up. "All right," she agreed. "I will go with you."

Liv smiled, leaning in to press another kiss to Amala's lips. Now she just had to get her parents to see, but she did not think that would be as easy as convincing Amala to come home with her.

Jorek and Bas had taken another road up the mountain, which explained why they had been ahead, coming towards them. They were now taking that road home, with Amala leading the way. She knew the Black Mountains like no one else, after all.

The tension between the four of them was palpable. Both Jorek and Bas seemed to be against Amala going with them, or perhaps it was the fact that she was something more to Liv than a friend, as they had obviously seen them kissing. They could not have missed it, and Liv knew both her brother and her familiar were quite protective of her, even when they were angry with her.

"Why are you travelling without guards?" Liv questioned, wanting to break the tense silence.

"We wanted to find you quickly, and the less people in our party, the better," Jorek replied tersely.

"I see." Liv bent her head, not knowing what else to say. Mother and Father had let Jorek off on his own, which was unusual. Jorek was a trained warrior, yes, but he always had at least two guards with him in the capital and fellow warriors with him when he travelled.

"I do not like this, Liv," Jorek spoke up softly.

Liv raised her head, looking over at him in wonder. She had not heard that tone of voice for many years ,that caring tone, the worried tone.

"I do not like that you plan on living a commoner's life," he continued, eyes trained straight ahead. "It is quite different than what you are used to, and even if you have been living like it for a short while... even if you like it now, you might grow to dislike it in the future."

"Jorek." Liv sighed. "I am lucky to have lived in the castle, in the luxury that we, as royals, have, but I do not want it and I do not need it. I know that. I will not come to resent my choice in the future. I will resent it more if I stay. Court life is not for me and it never has been. Can you just support my choice, even if you do not understand? We are not the same, Brother; we want different things in our lives. I do not second-guess your decisions. All I ask is that you do not second-guess mine. I am sure of this."

He finally looked at her, his eyes conflicted. "You are my little sister. I worry for you."

"I know, but I can take care of myself. And if for some reason I cannot, I have Amala to do it for me." She smiled as she thought of her first meeting with a lindworm, how she had frozen up and how Amala had come to the rescue.

Jorek's eyes flickered to Amala's back ahead of them for a moment, then settled back on Liv. "You care for the woman?"

Liv nodded. " I do."

"Good for you." He sounded completely sincere.

Liv watched him quietly. Of all her siblings, Jorek was the only one who still was not married. He was the next to youngest child, only two years older than Liv herself. As far as Liv knew, Jorek had no romantic entanglement going with anyone.

The sound of hooves brought Liv back to the here and now. She watched as Amala came riding back to her side. "This is lindworm territory," Amala told her. "They're all over the woods, but in this area there are more than usual. The trolls wandering around might have scared some away, but not all. So keep your eyes open and be alert."

Liv nodded gravely. Even if she had gone on this trip to help Amala slay the lindworms, she hoped she would not meet one again. Or a troll. She had had a lifetime's worth of trolls. She knew she would eventually have to deal with at least lindworms again if she wanted to stay with Amala, but for now... she could very well do without them.

Although, if something were to happen, maybe it would do something about the tension between the four of them. Amala was intent on scouting, Jorek was worrying and Bas... Bas was avoiding her, so he was probably sulking.

"I have had enough."

Liv put her hands on her hips, staring steadfastly at Bas. She had him neatly cornered now in a dark corner of the inn where they were staying. For four days she had let him sulk and avoid her, but she really had had enough.

"I get that you are angry with me for leaving like that and for now wanting to renounce my title," she started, "but this is my life, Bas. Even though I am the daughter of a king and queen, I do have a say in the matter."

"You are selfish, is what you are," he snapped, and Liv could clearly picture him in his cat-form, his fur standing on end in anger.

"How am I selfish?" she asked, her anger rising as well.

His eyes, the colour and shape of a cat's, glared at her. "Because you think only of yourself. Do you know, or even care, what I have had to give up for you?"

"No, I do not," Liv replied in frustration. "I cannot remember a time when you were not there. You have always been with me."

"I am a simple commoner," he replied, his anger fading to sudden nostalgia. "I had a good life, in the little village I grew up in. Then in comes a little princess whose heartbeat I can feel, and I am shipped to the capital to be properly educated. I have not seen my parents since and I have barely been allowed to send a letter every now and then."

He took a deep breath, eyes skittering past Liv. "It has not been easy for me, you know, staying at court. Nobles do not take kindly to a commoner being around them, especially not when that commoner is given the same education and the same status as them."

" I did not know," Liv replied faintly.

She truly had not. She had always thought Bas had been around the castle, though he had never spoken of any parents or siblings. Now he mentioned it... People back home did not care for Bas. He was never included in conversations unless he was with Liv, he had no other friends that she knew of.

"Bas, I am so sorry," she whispered. "No one ever told me anything. That is not an excuse, though, is it? I should have noticed how they treat you and demanded an answer. But I... I guess I am selfish because I have never really noticed how you are seen at court."

Bas crossed his arms over his chest and seemed to almost shrink into the dark corner. He was several years older than her, but right then he looked like a lost little kid.

"I think you should go home," she said then. "Go back to the life that was taken from you."

Bas raised his head, staring at her. "I am your familiar," he argued. "I took a vow to the King and Queen. I cannot just leave you. You have been my family for fifteen years."

Liv blinked. "Fifteen? I was five when we were bonded?"

Bas nodded. "And I was fourteen."

Liv stepped closer to him, putting a hand on his forearm. "Then, as I am still a princess of the realm, I am ordering you to go back home. I will deal with Mother and Father, do not worry. You just... go be happy, Bas. I know now you are not happy at court, and I doubt you will be happy travelling around the realm with me and Amala."

Bas looked torn and conflicted. "Are you sure of this, Liv?"

"We will always be bonded." Liv smiled. "But we do not have to be together. I have been away from you for a while now, and all has gone well. So go home. Go to where you really want to be."

Bas drew her into a hard, unexpected hug then. Liv let out a startled laugh, not used to this kind of affection, not from Bas. She wrapped her own arms around him, hugging him tightly.

"Just go," she told him, voice filled with emotion. "After fifteen years, you deserve to be happy."

"I have not been entirely unhappy," he muttered against her shoulder. "Not all the time."

"Good. I would hate for you to have spent the entirety of your fifteen years bonded to me unhappy." She sniffled as it finally dawned on her just how different her life would be now. She would not live in luxury, she would not have Bas, her bonded and tutor, around anymore, she would have nothing of what she was used to...

"I know I have been hard on you, but you have been good, Liv." Bas drew away, but he kept a hold of her upper arms still. "You are a strong woman and I have no doubt in my mind that you can do whatever you set your mind to."

He kissed her cheek, then brushed past her. Liv turned, eyes filling with tears, and watched as Bas disappeared up the stairs to his room. He came down only minutes later, his saddlebags slung over his shoulder. Liv watched as he crossed the inn and disappeared out the door.

Out of her life.

Her gaze was drawn to the other side of the room, where Amala was sitting at a table. She was not looking at Liv, her attention on the stew she was eating, but Liv felt warmth spread through her at the simple sight of Amala sitting there.

Her life would change, but she would be getting something new in it. Something new and exiting and promising. Someone more than a friend, someone who could be a lover, who would be at her side.

She would have Amala.

For now, that felt enough for her. She hoped it always would.

"Mother. Father."

Liv stood across from her parents, her hands folded behind her back to hide the nervous trembling. Jorek stood rigid at her side.

Mother's eyes went from one to the other. "Where is Bas?" she demanded to know.

"He has gone home," Liv replied, keeping her voice level and strong. "I sent him home."

Mother's eyes cut into her. "Why would you do that, child?"

"Because he has not been happy here." Liv stood rigid, having sworn to herself she would be strong throughout this. Her parents would not be happy with her, even less than they already were.

"So first you run off, and then when you are found, you send your tutor, your familiar, away?" Mother's voice was as cold as ice.

"Yes. I did." Liv nodded slightly.

"You are in so much trouble, Liv — "

"No, I am not," Liv interrupted. "I am here to renounce my title."

Both her parents looked like they had been hit across the face. Father schooled his features first, though Mother was not far behind. "What?" they both demanded.

"I want my life to be my own, and not for you two to do as you wish with it. I do not want to live in this castle, in this gilded cage. I want to travel the country, get to know the people, and actually have to work for my living." Liv set her jaw stubbornly, telling herself again and again that she was going to see this out. She was not going to cave for them.

Mother's eyes went to her youngest son. "Jorek. What is this nonsense?"

"It is not nonsense, Mother," Jorek replied, keeping his eyes downcast. "This is what she wants. I have never seen Liv as happy as she has been on our journey back. Let her have her way — or else she will run again, and this time I will not go after her. She will not come back a second time."

Liv felt extreme affection for her brother in that moment, but this was a bad time to show it, so she bit her lip, keeping her smile away.

"You want your sister to become nothing but a peasant?" Mother asked him incredulously.

"It is what she wants," Jorek pressed. "She is a different person than you are, Mother. If you try to force her into a life she does not want to live, she will resent you. Then neither of you will be happy."

Mother seemed to deflate a little, and she sighed as she looked back at Liv. "What are your plans then? What will you do?"

"I want to go into healing," Liv told her softly. "I will graduate and go into the field of healing. I want to be able to help people that are hurt. I have the talent for it. I really do." She cast a quick thought to Amala's thigh, knowing how well she had done with that job. She wanted to do more like that. Injuries such as the one Amala had suffered, the recovery time took months. Not to speak if they did not catch an infection and die. With Liv's help they'd be up and going right away.

Mother sighed heavily. She glanced over at Father. Father looked at Mother, then he sighed as well. "If that is the choice you make, Daughter," he spoke up for the first time. "Then so be it. Even if you do not bear the title of princess any longer, you will still be our daughter. If you need us, do not hesitate to ask."

"Thank you, Father." Liv bowed her head. "I really appreciate that."

Mother's head turned between Liv and Father. "Where will you live?"

"Here and there." Liv shrugged her shoulders. "We will be traveling around, helping people."

"You need a permanent residence that you can go home to when you need some rest," Mother insisted. "Travelling around without having a home... That is ridiculous. We will give you an estate, Liv, and you will take it graciously. We can talk more about it before you leave."

Liv nodded. "Thank you, Mother. That is very kind." She curtsied before leaving the room. She knew when she had been dismissed. Jorek did not follow, so he still wanted to talk to them. Or they to him.

She started towards her rooms, knowing Amala would be there waiting. She had left her there, polishing her sword, when she had been summoned to her parents. She had no doubt that Amala would still be there and still working on her sword.

As expected, Amala was sitting cross-legged on the floor, her sword lying across her thighs. She looked up when Liv entered, silver eyes intent. "How did it go?"

"Much better than expected." Liv smiled and sat down on the floor across from her, wanting to be on Amala's level instead of having to look down at her. "They want to talk to me later, but they will let me make my own choices. Their only condition was that they wanted to give me an estate, so that I would always have a home to go to."

"Where would that estate be?"

Liv shrugged. "I do not know. I guess that is a topic of conversation they want to have on a later date."

Amala sheathed her sword and put it to her side, then folded her hands and turned a solemn look on Liv. "I came with you, Liv, but I can't stay. Not for the time it will take for you to become a certified healer."

Liv bit her lip, knowing it had been coming. "It will only be a few months. I am about to graduate as it is. I'll have to settle in the healing path, which takes about four months. After that, I'll be allowed to go on my own, gather my own experience."

"I can't stay here for four months." Amala shrugged her shoulders. "Not even four weeks. I am not made to stay in a city—I can't stand them. I grew up in the wilderness close to the Trollheim."

"Trollheim?" Liv frowned.

"You call it the Jotun Mountains. We call it the Trollheim."

"So you are a Jotun?" Liv did not know if any Loreans had ever migrated to the other part of the Jotun Mountains, as there were no active description of Jotuns and their land in Lore.

"That is what your people call us, yes." Amala nodded. "I was a chieftain's daughter before I was banished. Now I'm just a lindworm hunter and I've got many people depending on me in the Black Mountains. I need to get back—it's summer and high season for the worms. I can't leave those people, those villages, to their own fate."

"I know." Liv did know. It did not, however, mean that she liked it. "I know you have to leave and that I have to stay here. But when I am done with my studying, in about four months time, I want us to meet up, because I do not want to lose you."

"You won't lose me." Amala leaned in, pressing a soft kiss to Liv's lips. "We will meet up when you've finished your studies. Then we can work on being a team."

Liv nodded, sniffling just a little bit. "You are willing to wait for me?"

"As long as I can go off to do what I do best, yes, I am willing. You go study to become a healer, so that you can help people your way, and I'll do it mine." Amala smiled slightly. "For four months, I'll go back to being by myself, which will be hard because I have grown accustomed to having you around. But I'll manage, because you'll be back eventually."

Liv spontaneously reached out and wrapped her arms around Amala, hugging her tightly. "I have come to care a great deal for you. I wish I could leave right away, I have become accustomed to travelling the woods, but I also need to do this if I shall be of any help to anyone."

"I understand that." Amala hesitantly put her own hands on Liv's back, and Liv knew by that action that Amala was not used to this kind of affection. "I'm fine with it."

"So when will you leave?" Liv asked, voice light.

"In the next few days," Amala replied.

Liv felt a lump form in her throat, and she quickly swallowed it. She smiled, not wanting Amala to see how upset she was by Amala leaving and being left here by herself. She did not even have Bas anymore. Of her many siblings, Jorek was the one she was closest to and he... well, he was not available most of the time.

"Then we will make the most of the few days we have left," she smiled, hoping it looked more positive than she felt. She knew she would be with Amala soon, but spending four months in the capital now, all alone, after all she had experienced... she did not look forward to that.

Amala smiled back, her eyes glinting. "Yes, we will."

epilogue

Four and a half months later

Liv urged her horse forward, into the little village where she and Amala had stayed after their first encounter with a troll.

There were only a handful of little houses, more like huts. The inn stood out right in the middle of them.

She has to be here, Liv thought, holding on tightly to the reins. They had agreed to meet in this little village, as this was the one experiencing the most lindworm attacks. Liv was half a month late, but Amala had to be there waiting for her.

Being back in the capital, being close to her parents and the court and studying at the university... it had her convinced that she would not miss that life. She would miss some of the luxuries, like her soft bed and always being able to take a hot bath when she wanted, but all in all ,she would not miss it much.

Eloy, the husband, was outside when she halted her horse in front of the inn. He peered up at her, hand going up to shield his eyes from the sun.

"Miss Liv!" He bustled over to take her horse. "Miss Amala has been waiting for many days now."

Liv could not help but smile at that. "I was delayed. But I am here now." She jumped down from the horse and took her saddlebags, then let Eloy take the mare away.

She heard the door open behind her and she turned slowly, expecting to see Eloy's wife, but hoping— "Amala!" She promptly dropped her saddlebags and threw her arms around Amala's shoulder as the woman came toward her.

"You're late," Amala told her sternly.

"I know and I am sorry. I was delayed from leaving by my parents. But I am here now." She pulled back so that she could look at Amala. She tangled her hands in the tiny braids, loving the feel of them twining in between her fingers. "I am here now," she repeated, staring into Amala's silver eyes. Her choice, to leave and to come here, felt absolutely right.

"Finally." So saying, Amala bent down to kiss her, a soft, caring kiss that made Liv's knees wobbly. When it intensified, and the world narrowed down to just the two of them, Liv felt with a certainty that her life was finally as it should be.

desert fire

about the story

When fires don't burn you, you seek out the hottest flames of all.

Brand is a warg, a wolf-shifter, and a fire mage, outcast and rejected by his people because of his true nature — and because he helped save a former friend.

Now, with no home, no family, no friends, and with an ability he doesn't understand, he doesn't know where he belongs. With nothing to loose, he heads to the land of the dragons to see if their fires are hot enough to burn him.

But once there he's taken prison and bought to the royal palace. There he meets someone special, someone who isn't afraid of him or who judges him, and Brand starts to believe that perhaps he can find a place to belong after all.

chapter one
prisoner

Why am I here?

Brand stared down at the dry ground beneath his feet, and then let his eyes roam the landscape ahead of him. The ground was dry and cracked for as far as he could see. Hills and mountains rose on the horizon, some giving off steam, a tell-tale sign that they were volcanoes.

Brand had never seen volcanoes before, only heard of them in stories. Stories about this dry, hot, wretched land he was currently standing on. Turning his head, he looked back the way he had come. The mountain range reached out on both sides, closing off this land from the one from which he had come. Trees could be still be seen, but they had thinned the closer he had come to what was called the Dragon Territories.

Why was he there indeed...

His eyes strayed to a group of three men, standing at a distance from him, conversing lightly. They were lowly criminals, crude and filthy, but he had needed them to get there. They had been there before — and he hadn't.

And as to the reason: dragons and volcanoes. Those were the reason he was there, standing on that dry land, eyes again going to the sky, looking for the mythical creatures the other three were there to hunt. Brand was also hunting, but his intention was not to kill. He just wanted... confirmation, so to say. Confirmation of what he was, of what he could do.

A dragon's fire... The lava of the volcanoes... Those were said to burn hotter than any bonfire. No fire had ever burned Brand and so he was there to see if the hottest of fires could do him harm. Because if it couldn't... he was what he was. If it could, he did not know what he was. Either way, he still could not go home.

"Hey lad, you plan on slaying dragons with that little dagger?"

Brand turned his head slightly, gazing down at the dagger attached to his belt. "I am not here to slay dragons," he revealed, taking several steps ahead. His horse followed him, stopping when he did.

"You are not slaying?" The man's voice got dangerously low. "Then what are you doing here?"

"I am merely curious." Brand hadn't exactly lied to them when he'd met them at an inn on the other side of the Black Mountains. He had overheard them talking about hunting dragons, and as dragons were said only to exist at the other side of the mountains, he had asked to join them. He hadn't said he wouldn't slay dragons, but he hadn't said he would either.

"Curious?" Brand heard boots stalk towards him. "What do you mean you're curious, you little—" He broke off as a big shadow fell over them.

Brand lifted his head and stared up at the creature blocking his view of the sky. He could not see much detail, but he could see the leathered wings beating powerfully to keep the big beast up in the air.

Brand felt his heart speed up, the excitement of seeing a real dragon overtaking him. Not that he could see much of it, as it blocked the sun, leaving itself in shadow, but there was no mistaking that outline. He had been shown a drawing of a dragon once and it had fascinated him.

When he had found out what he could do, it had fascinated him even more — even growing so far as to be an obsession. The obsession had grown after he had been banished from the pack, never allowed to go back, and after staying at Vortigern with Garrick and his strange friends.

He had not been able to stay there, though, so he had left in the dead of night when he had recovered, leaving only a short letter, and that was that.

The massive shape overhead beat its powerful wings again, but differently that time, and suddenly it descended, landing heavily on the hard, cracked ground several feet ahead of them.

It really was a big beast. White scales covered the entirety of its body, except for dark, leathery skin on its belly and feet. Its talons were easily as big as Brand's forearm, and looked sharp enough to rip through the dry ground on which it stood. They certainly would have no problem ripping through human flesh.

"A youngling," he heard the man behind him mutter, drawing up to Brand's side. "This one is not full-grown. Younglings aren't as valuable as full-growns, but valuable enough."

Brand did not know why the man was telling

him that, as he had just told them he was not there to slay dragons, but his words struck him nonetheless. If that huge creature was not full-grown, if it was just a youngling, then how big would a full-grown dragon be?

He swallowed, hoping fervently that he would not meet a full-grown dragon, but in the next moment he chastised himself. He was there for the dragons – or their fire. A dragon's fire was rumoured to be more vicious than any other fire, and seeing as Brand had never been burned, he was going to take his chances there, in that desert land known only for its warmth and its dragons and mountains that could spit fire.

Brand just wanted to belong somewhere. A realm of fire must certainly be a better place for him, who could manipulate it, than what he'd left behind.

A roar broke him out of his thoughts and Brand watched in horror as the men he had arrived with attacked the dragon – shooting arrows at its vulnerable feet, and thrusting spears towards its underside. The dragon drew back, flashing its teeth in another angry roar.

Brand stood frozen, not knowing what to do. The dragon was a wild beast, as likely to kill Brand as the three men with whom he had travelled. He wouldn't mind the men's deaths, he cared nothing for them and did not even know their names, but he preferred to keep his own life.

An arrow came out of nowhere, lodging in the chest of one of the men. He crumpled to the ground immediately, the arrow having pierced his heart.

Brand stared up at the sky and saw three big shapes high up. One of them dove; it was decidedly bigger than the one being attacked and with scales glinting a deep red. Atop its back sat a man, bow poised, an arrow having already lodged in the second man's chest.

Brand stared at the man, not able to help himself. He was well built, and the fact that he was wearing only breeches showed off his toned body extremely well. His skin was golden, evidence of time spent outside, and his hair was a golden brown.

The beat of wings around him snapped him from his perusal of the man riding the red dragon, and he turned to watch as the other two dragons he had seen in the sky landed on the ground, one a brilliant green, the other the color of the sky.

He noticed briefly that both had men atop

them. Another roar from the youngling dragon caught his attention, and he only managed to catch a flurry of movement in the corner of his eye before he dropped to the ground.

When he woke, it was dark. Not the dark of night, but the dark of a closed-off room deep in the ground. Brand could see nothing, but his aching back told him quite clearly that he was lying on a cold, hard stone floor. He groaned as he turned over, getting his knees under him and sitting up carefully. His head throbbed, clear evidence that someone had knocked him out over the head.

The fact that he could not see in the dark was probably supposed to terrify him, but Brand had means of seeing. His captors just did not know of them. A flame sparkled to life, hovering above his outstretched palm. Looking around, Brand saw that he was in a dungeon and that he was completely alone in his cell. He could not see or hear anyone in the other cells either.

He let the flame spark more to life, lighting up more of the dungeon. He had, through the years, mastered his strange ability and he had it completely under his control. The witch that

Garrick and his lover had shacked up with had offered to teach him, but Brand did not need teaching. He could control it already. All he needed was a place to belong...

He had not belonged back home, he had not belonged at Fort Vortigern... and seeing as he was locked in a dungeon, he was probably not ever going to be welcome there either.

All because he had opted to travel with dragon slayers.

Brand lay back down on the floor, his head hurting. There was nothing inside the cell but the floor, so there was nothing to ease his pain. The lacerations on his back twinged, reminding him of the brutal treatment he had got from the pack before he had been banished. All because of Garrick... it had always been all about Garrick.

Pushing the bitter thoughts away, Brand used his mind to control the flame, letting it soar over the floor. He had no purpose with it, but it helped him keep his mind occupied.

Voices from outside the dungeon startled him and the flame vanished in thin air just as the door creaked open. Brand lay still, dreading what was to come. It wouldn't be good, not when he was locked in a cell. At least they had not put him in chains.

He could make out the voices of three men, speaking in a tongue he had never heard before. As they entered the dungeon, he saw that each held a torch, bringing more than enough light to see by.

Brand sat up again, not wanting to be lying down when they got to him. He did not want to be sitting either, but he was not sure he could stand, so he just had to meet them like that.

One of them unlocked the cell and it creaked as he pulled the door open. He stepped inside, handing the torch over to one of his comrades as he did so.

Brand watched him silently, recognizing him from earlier. He was the one who had been riding the red dragon—and who had killed the other men he was with. Not that that was any loss, but it showed how ruthless he was. And Brand was their—

"Prisoner," the man spoke, and it startled Brand as he realized that the man spoke in his own tongue. "You are the only one of your comrades left alive, which is not a mercy, I assure you. We do not take kindly to dragon slayers."

Of course Brand had to be the only one left alive, the one to take the punishment for the other three whose profession he was not even a part of.

"I am not a dragon slayer," Brand said, determined to stand by his own truth.

He was backhanded fiercely. "Do not lie!"

Brand did not reach up to touch his cheek, though his hand itched to do so. The man was strong, he would give him that, because he had just tripled Brand's headache and his cheek throbbed painfully.

"I am not a dragon slayer," he forced out through clenched teeth. "I knew those men were, but they are no comrades of mine. All I wanted was to be shown the way here. I am not here to slay dragons."

"You lie!" One of the other two men said, stepping closer to him, his hands curling threateningly into a fist.

Brand stared at him, hard, not knowing what to do to convince them he was not there to harm the magnificent beasts. That he was only looking for a place to belong. He could not speak of that, of course, because it was none of their business, none but his own, and by the way they were acting, he would not find a place to belong there anyway, so better to just stay quiet.

The one closest, the one who had

backhanded him, straightened up, gaze cool as he regarded Brand. "We'll leave him be for now. With no food or water, I am sure he will soon speak the truth." So saying, he turned on his heel and stalked from the cell.

The other man glared at Brand, then came closer and hit him hard, sending Brand sprawling to the floor. The fist had broken his lip and his nose was bleeding, the taste something Brand was long used to. Not to mention the fists. The standing man kicked him hard in the gut as well, not content with just hitting him. Brand curled up, but refused to groan in pain—he would not give the bastard that much satisfaction.

He did not look up until the cell door creaked closed, and then only to roll over on his back. He was certainly no stranger to being beaten up, but he thought he was done with that since he had been banished. He had not thought he would be taken for a criminal and locked up in a dungeon in a strange country. He wondered what was awaiting him, because no matter what he said those men were convinced he was there to hurt their dragons, and they would see him punished for it.

Brand wiped the blood from his lip and nose,

ruining the sleeve of his tunic as he did so. Then he shifted into wolf-form and curled up, hoping to get some rest before the three men came back to torture answers out of him, because surely that was what they would do next when refusing him food and water did not work.

Brand was roused from his doze at the familiar creak of the cell door opening. He fervently hoped the three men were not back so soon, because he could not take being beaten much more. But he could not move his head to see who was joining him, because it all hurt so much. It hurt too much even to shift – because even in wolf-form the pain would be unbearable.

A cool cloth placed on his forehead startled his eyes open, and he turned his head a fraction to look at his visitor. It was not one of the three men who had been interrogating him earlier in the day, or perhaps it was the day before? No, it was someone else entirely. Not that Brand could see him, because the way he had placed his torch left his own face in shadow, but the gentleness of his hands as he washed away the blood on . Brand's face told him it just could not be one of them. Not after how he had been treated.

"They have certainly done a number on you," a low, soothing voice said. It was definitely masculine, so it was not a woman washing away his blood so carefully. "And yet you keep to your story."

"Because it is true," Brand rasped out, his throat sore from lack of water. "I am not here to hurt anyone, least of all your dragons." Though he could. He could hurt the men, even kill them, if he wanted to, but that would leave him a criminal for sure, and Brand just wanted to be left in peace.

"Then who are you?" the man asked gently. "You came here with dragon slayers. Those men almost killed a youngling and the riders cannot let that pass. You were with those men, so you had to be a part of it. It is very black and white with them."

Brand could hear some underlying bitterness in his voice, but he could not get himself to care for anyone but himself at the moment. His head throbbed, his body hurt, his throat was sore...

"I merely wanted to see the dragons," he rasped out. "Yes, I came with slayers and I knew the intent of their visit, but I only came here to see them. To see if..." He trailed off.

"See if... what?" the man pressed softly.

"To see if their fire can burn me," Brand replied, figuring he had nothing to lose by divulging that little piece of information.

"Burn you?" The man's voice was sceptical, and Brand understood, because how many could control fire with their minds?

Lifting one of his hands, figuring the man would take it better if he started the flame above his palm than in free air, he let it light up into a little ball, hovering only inches from his skin.

A sharp intake of breath came from the man. In the light of the little fireball, Brand could see him. He was dressed in light-coloured clothing — breeches, a tunic tied with a colourful sash and soft boots — and a head-cloth of the same light-coloured material covered his head so that Brand could not see his hair. His face was no chore to look at though, golden-toned skin the same as the other three he had met of the desert people, lines smooth yet masculine, eyes a deep, dark colour. His plump lips were currently parted as he stared at the ball of flame in Brand's hand.

"No fire can burn me," Brand told him, "because I control fire with my mind. But your dragons are said to have the most powerful fire in them, and I want to see what those flames can do to me."

The man's face suddenly set into a scowl. "You want to meet an angry dragon head on, just to feel its fire?"

"Yes." Brand would have nodded if he could, but his head hurt too much without moving, so he refrained from it. "I just need... I just need to figure out my place. Find somewhere to belong, because I have not met anyone like me before." For some reason, he felt it safe to divulge his real reason to the man.

"I have not either," the man replied. "Someone who can manipulate fire that way... no, not just manipulate, but create fire. It is magnificent." The man sounded truly to be in awe. "You are magnificent, to be able to do such a thing."

Brand couldn't help but let out a sad, bitter chuckle at that. No one had ever believed him magnificent... more of a weakling that needed to be beat into both submission and manhood. And as a punishment for something he could not help—something he had had no say in, whatsoever.

"I will speak to the King," the man said then. "Tell him your purpose. Only he can release prisoners of Commander Kamoor."

Commander Kamoor... that had to be the man who rode the red dragon. The one who was always in charge, but it was not he who had delivered the worst beatings, that was the other one. And the third, he always kept back at the cell door, never coming closer.

"Thank you," Brand whispered. "I really appr —"

The door slamming open and the sound of boots stalking inside broke him off. Brand vanished his flame, leaving them only in the light of the torch.

"Khatlah!" A familiar voice boomed out, and Brand felt his stomach knot in dread. The voice belonged to the one who had administered the most vicious beating.

The man beside him never seemed to lose his calm, though. He only turned his head, regarding the approaching man coolly. "Sakoptari. What is this, treating a man in such a way and leaving him?"

"He is a prisoner, little brother," the other man snapped. "A prisoner and a slayer." He came into the cell and jerked Brand to his feet. Brand almost lost his footing but managed to keep himself upright. It took a lot though, because his whole body still bore the evidence of his earlier treatment. "He will come with me, and if he does not confess to his crimes after today, he will nonetheless be executed."

"You cannot do this!" Khatlah yelled, following in the other's footsteps as he started to drag Brand with him towards the door. "He is innocent!"

Brand was roughly shoved to the floor as Sakoptari spun around to backhand Khatlah, who by his own words was his little brother. "You dare believe the words of a prisoner? Hasn't it occurred to you that he will say anything to be let free?"

"Hasn't it occurred to you that sometimes people speak the truth?" Khatlah countered. "That sometimes things aren't like you make them out to be!"

If Brand hadn't been hurting so much, and worrying about where he was being taken, that sentence would've greatly intrigued him. Injury and pain kept his own fate front most in his mind—and judging by Sakoptari's words, he was to be executed either way.

Khatlah was backhanded again and his brother hurled words at him in their native language, then he turned abruptly, grabbed a hold of Brand again and dragged him with him.

Brand was aware of Khatlah following after them, though he doubted there was much he could do for him. If Brand wanted to get out of whatever it was they had planned for him, he would have to do it himself, but if he did... he would have to get away somehow because surely they would not let him live then.

He was dragged through a hallway and they emerged out into bright sunlight. Brand watched in horror as a man stepped up to meet them, a man he had never seen before... and he was holding a whip.

No! He wanted to tear his eyes away, but found that he couldn't. They were locked on the ruthless tool, and the bright land around him faded to be replaced by a small clearing in the woods back home...

Brand grunted as he was being roughly tied to a tree, the rope digging into his hands and his arms, but not around his back. His back was free for...

He grunted as the whip at last connected with his back. He could feel his skin opening up at the rough material of the whip, could feel blood starting to trickle.

"Father!" he yelled out, in both pain and rage.

"You are no son of mine!" came the harsh reply, followed by another lash. "You told the traitor and the witch of our plans and they got away. This is all on you. Of course I should've known it would come to this — you never could take your eyes off of him when you were younger."

Brand squeezed his eyes shut as his father's words seemed to strike him even more painfully than the whip.

"You are weak!" A lash punctuated it, but Brand clenched his teeth, refusing to let any sound out. "Weak and pathetic, just like your mother! I never should've agreed to take you in, to raise you properly. It was obvious from the start you would become nothing!"

After that, Brand could remember little else. All he knew was that the whip lashes eventually stopped, that they untied him and threw him away with a warning of what would happen should he ever return. And after that... he just let the blackness take him.

Brand was jerked back to reality as he was shoved forward, finding himself once again sprawled on the ground. He lay for a moment, feeling the hot, dry ground under his hands. The warmth of it did not bother him — because Brand was used to being warm. Controlling fire as he did left him constantly warm, as if he suffered from a never-ending fever.

The powerful beat of wings had him looking up, and he forced himself up on his knees as he watched the red dragon descend, its rider jumping down from its back the moment it landed to stride over to Sakoptari and Khatlah. He was dressed much the same as Khatlah — only his clothes were black and lacked the colourful sash.

"What is going on here?" he demanded, his voice hard and strong and used to being obeyed.

"I am getting a confession out of this mongrel," Sakoptari told him, turning away from Khatlah to face the man — who could be none other than the Commander Kamoor — straight on.

"Have you not beaten him enough?" the Commander demanded, his voice going stone cold.

Brand pushed himself up to his feet, swaying uncertainly for a moment, but managing to regain his balance. He hurt so much, but he could not stay on the ground anymore. He could not seem as weak as he felt.

"If the prisoner has not confessed yet, he never will," the Commander continued. "He should be given a fine and be sent on his way, because he did not actually try to kill the youngling."

Sakoptari made a sound of outrage, then he abruptly turned around and snatched the whip out of the servant's hands. His cold eyes locked on Brand and he swung his arm, releasing the whip—

Brand let his power course through him and the whip caught fire before it was even halfway towards him. He let the fire travel up the length of it until it reached Sakoptari's hand, and he promptly released the whip with a cry of pain.

"You can beat me and kick me," he groaned out between clenched teeth, "and treat me like scum. But you will never whip me!"

Four pairs of eyes were on him, and Brand subsided, letting go of his peculiar power, feeling it retract—but it was still there, lying in wait, pulsing for the next time he would use it...

Commander Kamoor strode forward and roughly grabbed a hold off Brand's chin, forcing his head up to meet his eyes.

"Your eyes. They are strange. And they were even stranger a moment ago." He used his bruising hold to tilt Brand's head, as if he could get a better look of his eyes that way. "What are you, to possess such peculiar eyes?"

"Do not care about his *eyes*!" Sakoptari snarled. "He just *attacked* me—he should be put in chains and executed to dare do harm to the crown prince!"

Brand's eyes widened slightly in surprise and he let them flicker just the briefest moment to the man that had caused him the most harm. He was the crown prince?

"You deserved it," Khatlah snapped, the contempt loud and clear in his voice. "I told you he was innocent and yet you continued to want to harm an already hurt man! I will not stand for this behaviour, and I use my authority as prince to declare this man my own personal guest for the foreseeable future, and to demand that no one harm him again." His eyes stared coldly at Sakoptari, but they also strayed briefly to the Commander still holding Brand's jaw in his bruising grip.

Sakoptari stared furiously at him, then snorted in contempt and stalked from the yard.

Grateful to see his back, Brand let his tension ease the tiniest bit.

Khatlah turned his full attention to him then, his eyes seeming to blaze in anger. "Let him go, Kamoor."

Kamoor did as told, letting go as roughly as

he had grabbed Brand, and turned to contemplate Khatlah, whom he seemed to tower over. "What are you trying to accomplish by keeping a foreigner in our midst? What do you think he will do when he goes running back home to the other side of the mountains? Our code is to never accept foreigners into our lands unless they swear an oath to never leave them, or have you forgotten that in your infatuation with this strange man?"

Khatlah did not answer, just kept staring coldly at the Commander. Kamoor cast one last, lingering look on Brand, then he too stalked from the yard, going inside what Brand realized was a palace.

And quite the magnificent one at that. Made of stones he could not identify, but which held a golden colour in the bright light of the sun. It was easily four stories high, the towers several more. It spanned out to both sides and surrounded the courtyard they were currently standing it. The sheer beauty of it could leave a man breathless — and Brand had never seen anything like it before.

The Vortigern Castle was magnificent in its own way, but the palace was sheer beauty.

Lowering his head, Brand looked around to

see that the Commander and the crown prince were really gone, then cast a curious glance at Khatlah, who was regarding him in silence.

Brand swallowed, the pain piercing into him even more without the threat to his life to distract him. Before he had only been aware that he hurt—every little cut, scrape and bruise was making itself known. Even those on his back, which were supposed to be healed, throbbed in pain.

He fell to his knees, knowing they got scraped on the hard, rough ground, but unable to care as all the other pains he felt hit him with full force. It was almost exactly like when he had been whipped, then thrown into the woods to die—only the pain then had been even worse. But the fact that he had experienced worse did not mean what he felt didn't affect him.

He was barely aware, as he collapsed on the ground, of someone shouting in the distance. The only thing he wanted was the darkness— and it came willingly.

chapter two
guest

Brand blinked his eyes open before quickly closing them again as the bright light seemed to pierce through him.

He lay quietly, eyes still closed as he tried to will away the hurt of the light. He could feel he was lying on something soft, which meant that he had definitely not been put back into the dungeon.

Easing his eyes open more carefully, he saw that he was in a room, decorated with light-coloured curtains and wall hangings.

Brand sat up slowly, feeling every ache in his body. But he did not hurt as much anymore, there were only the sore aches of healing. He realized that he was lying in a bed, not the kind of raised bed he was used to, but on a sleeping pad, surrounded by a myriad of pillows and blankets.

Looking down on himself he saw he was naked, save for the white fabric wrapped tightly around his torso, to keep his ribs in place, he guessed. He looked around, hoping to locate his clothes, but they were sadly absent. There was however, a neatly folded bundle at his side.

Shaking the various pieces of clothing out he started donning them, not wanting to be naked if someone were to come for him. It was exactly like the clothing both Khatlah and the Commander had worn the day before, except where theirs had been light and dark, Brand's was a warm shade of brown, completed with an orange sash.

Brand left the headpiece folded on the floor, not comfortable with the thought of wearing it. The Commander had not worn a headpiece either, nor had that bastard that had tried to whip him, so Brand counted on it not being a necessity.

The room he was in was oddly bare, save for the wall hangings and the bed pallet, giving heed to the fact that it was a room for guests. Brand moved stiffly over to the window, which was the source of the bright light inside the room as the sun shone straight through it.

He looked down into a courtyard—not the one where he had been—but a bigger one. Servants hurried across in all directions, and directly ahead was a big building that could be nothing but the stable, judging from one man trying to wrestle a horse inside.

Brand heard footsteps outside, and he turned in time to watch as the door opened. Khatlah stepped into the room, holding a tray with what could only be food, by the smell of spices.

"Ah, you are finally awake." Khatlah smiled slightly, closing the door behind him. He crossed over to the mat in the middle of the room, setting the tray down in front of him. "Come eat."

Brand went over to him reluctantly and sat down, eyes only for the tray. It held quite the amount of food. He could not say what it all was but it looked and smelled delicious, so he started in on it, not asking in case he did not want to know the answer. The customs there were quite different than back home, of that he was certain.

"How long have I been asleep?" he asked curiously.

"A day straight," Khatlah told him. "They really did a number on you, those idiots. They will be reprimanded when they are shown that you are no threat. Though Sakoptari tried to convince everyone otherwise, especially after you burned his hand."

Brand bowed his head back over the food. "I did not mean to, but I could not let him use that whip on me."

"I know." Khatlah voice was strangely filled with emotion. "I saw those lacerations on your back, when I undressed you and treated you. I am sure there is quite the story behind them, but I can also see that they are quite fresh, so I shall not ask."

"It is nothing much, really," Brand murmured. "My father did not like me warning an old friend of what they had planned for him and had me first punished then banished for it."

"That was quite cruel, for only telling your friend," Khatlah commented.

Brand did not say anything, just continued to eat. He had told Garrick what the pack had planned for him and the witch staying with him... and for that he'd paid dearly. He had always wanted his father to acknowledge him, be proud of him. Had wanted it so much he had stopped speaking to Garrick altogether—after being beaten up for looking at him intently, that was.

Brand's father would not allow his son to be starry-eyed over another male and for that Brand had been forced to cut out his only friend. His only friend, whom he had eventually saved from the wrath of the pack, then from a vicious lindworm.

Garrick had taken him with him to his new residence at Fort Vortigern, and there he had stayed until he had healed, but he did not belong. Garrick had his witch, and the two residents of the castle were too busy training the first two. The witch Lorcan had offered to teach Brand as well... but Brand could not stomach staying there.

So he had left in the dead of night, leaving only the letter for Garrick. Not that it would tell him much, but hopefully enough for Garrick not to worry. Perhaps he would see him again one day, and maybe when that day came it would not hurt anymore, but it was a long way ahead in the future yet.

Forcing those thoughts away, he focused on his current situation. "So what is to be done with me now?" he questioned.

"That is entirely up to you," Khatlah told him. "I spoke to Father, told him your story and he cleared you. You are my guest, you are free to walk about as you wish, and your life is your own. No one here can tell you differently."

Brand sighed. "Your people will not accept me," he spoke up, but did not look at Khatlah as he did so. "Not after the way I arrived here, as a prisoner. Not after being accused of killing dragons. I do not understand much about your people but I do understand that slaying dragons is an extremely offensive crime in your realm."

"It is." Khatlah bent forward slightly, eyes intent upon Brand. Brand noticed then that Khatlah was still wearing a head-cloth, not one tuft of hair sticking out, and it was of the same light-coloured material as the last time he'd seen him, setting off his tanned, smooth skin and his dark, striking eyes. "But you did not commit that crime. You are innocent and the people who matter know that."

"Your brother will not see it that way." Brand met Khatlah's gaze straight on.

"Sakoptari is in no position to argue it." Khatlah's voice spoke of finality. "Father has cleared you and now you are my personal guest. He will not like it, but it will keep him away. Because if he misbehaves too badly, Father can just as easily chose another heir, and I can promise you that that is something Sakoptari wants to avoid at all costs."

Brand frowned. "The king can just chose another heir if he so sees fit?"

Khatlah nodded. "If he does not think his current heir can handle ruling the realm, he is in his full right to choose another, whom he thinks can. It is our custom. It has rarely been done, usually the first-born takes the throne, but it is not uncommon for it to happen either. No one would protest, or talk too much about it, if it were to happen."

Brand subsided, thinking about how different the desert country was than back home. As far as he knew, the first-born always took the throne in Lore, no matter what—he had never heard otherwise. But then his old village was secluded, and he had never heard much of the outside world, but from the looks of the people, the dragons existing—dragons they rode... The desert was nothing like home. Nothing at all.

Khatlah sat back as well, his posture relaxing as he watched Brand eat the rest of the food on the tray. "I find I am still missing your name," he spoke suddenly, as if it had just occurred to him.

"I am Brand," Brand introduced himself, straightening up as he swallowed the last drops of wine in his cup. It had been good to have a proper meal for once, especially as he had been denied it in the dungeon.

"I am Khatlah, youngest prince of four." He held out his hand, and Brand took it hesitantly, shaking. "That is the way of greeting in your realm, is it not?" Khatlah wondered.

Brand nodded slightly. "What is your way of greeting?"

Khatlah bent forward so fast Brand only managed to blink and placed one soft kiss on each of his cheeks. Sitting back down, Khatlah smiled softly. "That is our proper way of greeting."

"You greet strangers like that?" Brand asked incredulously, taken aback by such an intimate gesture.

"You have experienced the greetings of a foe," Khatlah replied, "but now you are a friend."

Nodding, Brand looked everywhere but at Khatlah.

"I have duties to attend." Khatlah stood, then bent down to pick up the tray. "But I will see you this evening. Meanwhile, feel free to roam the palace, make yourself familiar."

Brand looked over at him then, catching the brief smile flitting over Khatlah's lips, then he turned and left the room. Brand sat still on the mat, thoughts flitting from one thing to another to a third, never quite settling on anything to ponder more deeply. Sighing, he got up and strode over to the door. He might as well take Khatlah up on his words — to roam the castle. It wasn't like he had much else to do.

Not really wanting to meet lots of people, Brand opted to go up the grand staircase, and not down, when he reached it. It was beautifully done, wide, set in gold and ascending the four stories of the palace. Brand followed it up to the fourth story, hoping that there would not be too many people on the top floor. There was only a small room, however, and right across him an ornate door.

Shrugging to himself, Brand went over and opened it, recoiling at the brightness of the sun as it was revealed. Blinking his way through the momentary blinding, Brand stepped outside. The palace proper was just three stories — the fourth was the roof. And on the roof there were... dragons.

Brand stared, eyes wide at the creatures in front of him. He stepped outside, letting the door shut behind him. The dragons had the whole roof of the main wing, except where buildings had been set up at the four corners, at the base of the towers. The wings that surrounded the main one were four stories high, creating a wall so that the dragons couldn't possibly be seen from the ground. Thus why Brand had not seen them when he had been in the courtyard.

The dragons were too big to fit inside the buildings, so Brand guessed they housed food and gear. There weren't many dragons on the roof, that would've been impossible no matter how big the roof was, but the few that were there were scattered, most of them asleep.

Brand's eyes fell on a red dragon, which was the only one not lying down. It looked back, its yellow eyes cold and ruthless. It was a predator, a dangerous one, and it was the dragon of the Commander — Brand could not forget the sight of the magnificent beast. His eyes slid away and saw that several feet behind the red dragon lay the one that had been hurt by the three men with whom he had travelled.

Brand swallowed, and then slowly started making his way towards it. The red dragon followed his every move, poised as if to attack at the slightest motion. Brand looked at it from the corner of his eye. The dragon was full-grown—

the hurt youngling was nothing compared to it.

Reaching the youngling, Brand crouched down. Its wounds were bound and it was breathing properly, so he hoped it would make a successful recovery. It was currently asleep, its head resting on the ground, eyes closed.

Movement from behind brought his head up and he groaned in pain as he was roughly dragged to his feet and pushed up against the wall surrounding the entire roof. Blinking to clear his sight, he stared right into the scowling face of the Commander.

"What are you doing on the roof?" he demanded.

"Khatlah said I could roam the palace," Brand explained, his hand gripping Kamoor's arms, hoping fervently he would not choke him because Brand was not strong enough to fight him. "I mean no harm. I am merely curious."

"Curious, indeed." Kamoor reached up to tilt Brand's head just so, staring into his eyes, just as he had done the other day. "Eyes like yours... I have seen them before."

Brand frowned.

"They are exactly like the eyes of the wolf-creatures that reside in the woods," Kamoor continued. "Why do you bear the eyes of such a creature?"

Brand saw no reason to lie; it would only make it worse for him. "Because I am a shifter. You know the tongue I speak, surely you must also know that there are shifters on the other side of the mountain."

"I have heard stories." Kamoor pressed him more firmly against the cool wall, tilting his head the other way. "If you can indeed shift into the wolf-creature, and if you as human share its eyes, is it safe to say that you share other traits with it as well?"

Brand frowned, not understanding what Kamoor wanted from him.

"Like, say, the sense of smell?"

"I do not understand," Brand spoke.

"Do you have a better sense of smell than anyone else?" Kamoor asked sharply.

"I..." Brand was taken aback by the question. "I do not know. I was born like this, this is normal for me. I do not know if your sense of smell is better or worse than mine. I do not know if you can see better or worse than me, because I have always been like this and I know nothing else."

"I think it is safe to say that you do." Kamoor's tone of voice did not change, but

Brand had the strange feeling that he was satisfied by it.

"Why do you want to know?" Brand demanded.

"The men you came here with are not the only ones," Kamoor told him quietly. "They are part of a larger group of men here to kill our dragons and take them to the other side of the mountain, where we know not what happens to them. We patrol the woods, but have not been able to locate them while they stay hidden in the mountains. So we need something, someone, who is used to the woods and can find them easily. And what someone better than you, who has the eyes and senses of a creature of the woods?"

Brand wasn't sure he had heard correctly. "You want me to... help?"

"We need an advantage," Kamoor replied stonily. "Every day they kill more dragons. Mostly younglings and yearlings who do not have the experience or defences of the adults. We need our dragons. We rely upon them — and they rely upon us."

"Your comrades will not like my help," Brand pointed out, thinking about one man in particular. One that apparently happened to be the crown prince.

"Sakoptari may be above me in daily life," Kamoor said, "but amongst the dragon riders, I am in charge and he will do as I say. And if you are not here to kill our dragons, as you claim, you will help us get rid of those that are."

Brand nodded hesitantly, but it was enough, because Kamoor let him go. Brand sagged against the wall, hand going up to his neck. Kamoor's grip had been hard and steady, but he did not think he'd have bruises. He hoped not. It was worse with his ribs, they were sore and tender after being squished against the wall.

"When will we be leaving?" he questioned.

"When the current patrol comes back bearing news, we will act according to what they have to share. There is no saying however, when they will be back. We will just have to wait." So saying, Kamoor turned on his heel and stalked off.

Brand stared after him, watching that straight back, how his black clothing stretched across his broad shoulders... Shaking his head, Brand turned and found himself meeting the eyes of the red dragon. It stared back at him for a long minute, then it turned its head away and lay down, its back firmly to Brand.

Looking back at the youngling, who was still firmly asleep, Brand sighed and stalked off as well, going back the way he had come. His life was becoming complicated again—and he could not make up his mind on if it was a positive kind of complicated, or a negative one...

"How do you know my language?" Brand asked Khatlah, trying to distract himself from the awkwardness of the looks he was getting in the banquet hall. "We know nothing about your people, back home."

"You are not the first to cross the mountains with honest intentions," Khatlah told him. "Some of your people have come here, seeking shelter, a different life. We have given it to a few of them, those that vow to never return to what they left. And in return they have taught us their language."

Brand cast a quick look around at everyone gathered in the enormous hall, but he could see no one with the look of his own country. The colour of their skin varied greatly, but none were as pale as Brand—and he had thought himself quite tan back home. And everyone had slightly tilted eyes, nothing all like the rounded shape of his own. No one shared the colour of his eyes either, because none were shifters.

In that, he was all alone and no one knew, because he did not really want it spread. Unless the Commander was prone to gossip — which he highly doubted — it would not be known unless he himself chose to share it.

Khatlah had come to his room earlier in the evening, bearing a new set of clothes that he was to wear to the banquet being held. They had eaten, and people were milling about and talking. Brand, who was feeling anything but comfortable, was hiding away in a corner with Khatlah, who had followed him willingly.

"You really should mingle," Khatlah told him. "Get acquainted."

"I see no point in it," Brand murmured. "It is not like I am going to stay here for very much longer..." He did not know what was to happen with him after he helped locate the rest of the dragon killers, but he highly doubted that he would be let back into the palace. He was a lowly wolf-shifter and firewitch from across the mountains, so far out of his element he could drown in it. Not that there was anything to drown in — there were only wide stretches of dry, oftentimes cracked, ground or dunes of sand.

Khatlah's small smile faded, his eyes boring into Brand's. "You are leaving?"

Brand shrugged helplessly. "I do not know. My life is a mess and I do not know anything. All I know is that I am here now, but come tomorrow..." He let the sentence hang, knowing Khatlah would understand what he had trouble finding the words to say.

Khatlah turned away, but Brand caught the flash of disappointment in his eyes. "Will you follow me back to my room?" Brand asked tiredly. "I am not sure I will find it on my own."

Khatlah nodded, then led the way out of the banquet hall. He did not speak, and Brand found that he did not like the silence stretching on between them.

"I do not understand how you can be disappointed in me," he spoke up. "I do not belong here, and I have only been here for a few days. There is nothing about me that fits in here. Even amongst my own kind I am peculiar."

Khatlah's tension seemed to ease slightly, and he slowed down so that he and Brand could walk side by side. "I am disappointed because I thought I had gained a friend, only to find out that that friend is not planning to stay."

Brand swallowed the big lump suddenly getting stuck in his throat at the words. "You should not want to be my friend. I am only trouble, a peculiar creature that not even Lorcan can put a label on. And if Lorcan cannot—" He stopped abruptly, not wanting to go down that bitter road. Another reason he had left Fort Vortigern.

"What do you mean? Why are you so peculiar? You look just like any normal foreigner to me, except those strange eyes and those powers."

"Exactly!" Brand exclaimed. "I am a warg, a wolf-shifter, and that is all I am supposed to be. Yet I am also a firewitch. It does not make sense! Shifters only have the magic to shift, but they bond to witches to balance out their powers, though gaining nothing of their own except that bond. And here I am, both shifter and witch, and I know not what to make of myself, what to do with myself."

"Maybe you are just gifted," Khatlah replied. "Like no one has been before you. Gifted with both sets of magic, incapable of being bound to anyone in particular. Maybe you are supposed to make your own fate, instead of getting bound to some witch's." Khatlah stopped in front of

Brand's door, turning to face him. "And who is Lorcan?"

Brand caught the slightest hint of anger and suspicion in that voice, and before he could stop to think he took a step forward, pinning Khatlah to the door, and kissed him. Khatlah gasped in surprise, but quickly subsided, his hands coming up to grip Brand's shoulders. Brand had never kissed anyone before, but instinct drove him as he tilted Khatlah's head to the side, taking the kiss deeper.

They were pressed together, no space between them, and they seemed to get even more entwined as the kiss continued. Khatlah's arms slid around Brand's torso, one gripping his shoulder still, the other traveling up to tangle in his hair. Brand kept his own arm firmly around Khatlah, the other crept up to cup the back of his neck, the soft feel of the head-cloth under his fingers instead of the hair he really wanted to feel.

This is it, he thought, dazed. *This is what I've been looking for.*

"Khatlah!"

Brand broke away from the kiss at the angry voice, and he watched as Khatlah ran the back of his hand over his lips, almost guiltily, before looking up, dread in his eyes. Brand followed his gaze and watched as Kamoor stalked towards them, his eyes burning in anger.

"You just can't help yourself, can you?" he snapped, shoving Khatlah away from Brand and into the wall next to the door. "Helping yourself to the handsome stranger, huh?"

"You have no right," Khatlah forced out through clenched teeth. "No right to interfere in my life! You gave me up a long time ago and you cannot be mad at me for moving on!"

Brand took a step back and found himself with his back flush up against his door. He stared hard at the ground, wishing suddenly that they would just have their argument in their own tongue, instead of keeping to the custom of speaking a language everyone present could understand. He felt like an interloper, no matter that Khatlah had kissed him back because Brand had kissed him first. And apparently he had had some relationship with the Commander in the past, and Brand had thoroughly pissed off the man who had asked for his help, the man who held Brand's fate in his hands. Because a lot could happen on the mountain, and no one could argue if he had been killed in a so-called accident... or if they said he really had been out to get their dragons. No matter what he chose to say, the people would believe it and there was nothing Brand could do about it.

Kamoor kept Khatlah pinned, eyes still burning in anger and his breathing slightly sped up, but he eventually let Khatlah go with a snort of contempt then turned to face Brand. Brand did not back down from that cold stare, because he could not show any weakness in front of Kamoor — that would certainly be the death of him.

"The scout patrol is back. We leave at dawn."

It took a few moments for the words to make sense, for the surprise at not being yelled at or beaten to register. Brand nodded, his gut clenching painfully at the various scenarios of the trip running through his mind.

"What?" Khatlah's head moved from Brand to Kamoor and back to Brand again. "What is going on? Where are you going?"

"He will be helping us for a little while," Kamoor told him coldly. "If he wants to come back after... that is up to him. It would not be for you though, that much I can assure you." With that, Kamoor turned and walked off, not looking back once.

Brand looked at Khatlah, who seemed

stricken. He had a hard time catching his breath, and his eyes were filling up. If that had been someone back home, Brand would not have a single care, but it was Khatlah... the only one to be nice to him, and whom he had just kissed, for some reason he did not want to dwell upon.

"Come on." Brand wrapped an arm around Khatlah's shoulder and guided him into Brand's room. Khatlah's breathing became worse, and he bent over when Brand let go of him to close the door, gasping for breath. "Breathe," Brand told him, going over to him and kneeling on the floor so that he could see Khatlah's tear-stained face. "Come on, just breathe. Calm and steady."

Khatlah's eyes locked on his and he did as Brand told him, taking first a shaky breath, then another until he had calmed down. The tears however, did not want to stop and they started trickling faster as he got his breathing under control.

Brand pulled Khatlah down to the floor and into his arms, holding him tightly as Khatlah cried. "I know we are almost strangers, but if you want to talk I am here," he whispered. "I am not good at this sort of thing, but I promise I will try."

Khatlah sniffled, then burrowed his head

further against Brand's neck. "Kamoor and I were never lovers," he started, his voice trembling. "We never got that far. We kept dancing around each other, very much in love. Then one day, out of the blue, he suddenly accused me of... of..." Khatlah could not continue, but Brand could very well understand just what he had been accused of, by their argument outside. "But I did not do what he accused me of, I did not! And I do not know where he ever got that notion, because the man he accused me of being with was only passing through and I had only exchanged a single word with him." He shook in Brand's arms, his tears wetting Brand's clothes and skin.

"You are still in love with Kamoor," he commented, the only thing he could think of saying.

Khatlah nodded against him, a sob escaping him. "But I like you a lot, too. I really do."

"It is no matter, because Kamoor is still in love with you."

"He hates me," Khatlah countered. "After that... he has not been able to be in the same room as me. So he is not in love with me, he hates me. He will never look at me the same again because of that time, and I did not even do anything! I am hated for something I did not do, for some low lie someone has fed him. Why would someone do something like that?"

Yes, why would they? Brand rested his chin against Khatlah's head, the material of the head-cloth soft against his cheek. "Sometimes people act like they hate a person when they really don't. They act like they hate them because they have no other choice or because they know no other way to act. But the real feelings can be quite the opposite."

Brand should know that better than anyone. How many years had he treated Garrick like crap, only because he was afraid of his father? How much grief had he caused Garrick for all those years, just because he had been too terrified to tell him the truth? He had been such a bastard... It was a wonder Garrick had even bothered to take him with him to Vortigern at all after Brand had dealt with that lindworm.

And yet Brand had continued to be a bastard afterwards. He had avoided Garrick, had not wanted to talk to him... because he couldn't. Because Garrick had another lover, the witch he was bound to, and there was no space for Brand in his new life. So Brand had left. He had to get away — get his own life. Get over Garrick, once and for all.

And just when he thought he might've found what he needed... it turned out that that person was still in love with someone else, someone who treated him like crap. Someone so like what Brand had used to be.

chapter three
wolf

Khatlah pulled away when he had calmed down, and he looked up at Brand searchingly. His eyes were still wet, his face bore clear evidence of his crying, and yet Brand still wanted to kiss him so badly.

"You speak like you have experience," Khatlah commented, the desire for Brand to share his story clear in his voice.

"I have," Brand replied. "Except I was the bastard in my story, the one acting like Kamoor does towards you now."

"Was this towards this Lorcan?"

Brand couldn't help but smile slightly at that. "No, Lorcan is... he is a very powerful witch, and he has a lover whom he has been with for a very long time. No, my friend's name is Garrick. He's a shifter, like me; we were part of the same pack.

But my father did not approve of my friendship with him, and I... I was too afraid of what he would do to me. So I distanced myself, stopped talking to him, and when I did I was not kind. Garrick really thought I hated him. He probably still does."

"You never made amends?"

"No." Brand shook his head. "He tried talking to me after I warned him to get out of the village. The pack did not like that he had gone and got himself bound to a witch. I was severely punished for warning him, then banished. Garrick brought me back to the fortress, Lorcan's fortress. But I... Garrick had fallen in love with his witch, and I would cause him nothing more than grief by being there, for I just could not like his lover, even though he seemed really sweet. So once I was healed, I left."

Khatlah's hand was suddenly at his jaw, caressing his face softly. When Brand looked up at him, Khatlah bent forward so that their foreheads rested together. "So you claim Kamoor does not hate me, that he in fact is still in love with me."

"I do." The words hurt coming out, but Brand could not lie. He had lied almost all his life, he could not do it anymore. "I am absolutely certain of it."

Khatlah closed his eyes, squeezing them shut as if he were in pain. But his fingers did not stop caressing Brand's face, and Brand revelled in the soft feel of them ghosting along his skin.

"What are you helping Kamoor with?" Khatlah asked then. Brand could not say if he changed the subject for distraction or if he was genuinely curious.

"To locate the rest of the slayers," Brand told him quietly.

Khatlah drew a shaky breath, then pulled away. His eyes fell on the bed pallet. "Can I stay here with you tonight? Just... stay. In case you do not come back, I want... just to be with you tonight."

Brand nodded and they moved over to the bed pallet, both lying down on their backs, with suitable space between them. The silence stretched on, but suddenly Khatlah rolled over, resting his head on Brand's chest.

"I have been lonely for so long," he whispered. "Before I was always with Kamoor, then when he... I was all alone after that. I do not make friends easily, even being a prince. They all think me too weird."

"Why would they think you weird?" Brand

asked, frowning. Khatlah seemed no different than anyone else he had seen around the palace.

"Because I have no interest in the matters of state, or becoming a dragon rider, or getting married and raising a family. I do not belong in one certain group. Kamoor belongs to the riders, so does Sakoptari, though when he takes the throne he will become king. My brothers are all nicely settled down. I am the only one unattached, with no goal I am working towards and that makes me unusual, someone they cannot understand, and in a society where everyone is always working towards something... it is considered weird not to be working towards anything."

"But why?" Brand questioned. "Is there nothing you want to do?"

"I always only wanted to be with Kamoor," Khatlah replied, then he stiffened for a moment before he broke out into hysterical laughter. "I am so pathetic, aren't I?" he managed to get out through his laughter. "Pining away for that man for so long!"

Brand couldn't say much, he had been exactly the same and he could see what Khatlah saw in the Commander. He was a handsome man. Tall and with a nicely built, toned body, his skin a deep golden colour, attesting to the time he spent outside in the sun. His features were sharp and angular, and though every time Brand had seen him they had been set into a scowl, it did not make him look any less handsome.

"We should sleep," he said, his voice sounding hoarse to his own ears. "Apparently I am leaving early in the morning."

Khatlah stiffened against him. Then he turned away, putting his back firmly to Brand. "Yeah."

All kinds of emotions roiled behind that simple word, but Brand could not focus on Khatlah long enough to figure it out. Khatlah would have Kamoor, because they had to figure out their shit sometime, and Brand... he would probably move on. Maybe he should try the Jotun Territories, see if he had any more luck making a new life for himself there.

He had thought briefly that he could've made one in the desert, but his only friend, whom he had not known for long but found himself to be extremely attracted to, was in love with someone else. And Brand just could not live with that heartache again. That would be like going back to Vortigern and living with Garrick and his little earthwitch. It was something he just could not do. Not again. And this desert country... it didn't matter if a dragon's fire could burn him or not, because he could not stay here. Not when the situation was what it was.

So it was better to cut his ties, when said ties were as fresh as they were. They both would heal better that way. At least he hoped they would.

Kamoor stood in the open space in front of the palace's front door, his eyes boring into Brand as he exited the cool building to walk out into the burning sun. Kamoor's dragon stood behind him, its eyes, too, following Brand as he approached them.

He was flanked on both sides by Sakoptari and the other man who had been to the dungeons with them, the one that had mostly stayed by the cell door. They were also standing in front of their respective dragons.

No other people were around, only those three. They were all dressed in the manner Brand had come to recognize as standard for this desert, only the colours of their clothing varied. Kamoor's clothes were black, Sakoptari's were sand-coloured, as were those of the last man, whose name Brand did not know.

Brand was dressed exactly the same as the day before. A new set of clothes had been by his bed when he woke, but Khatlah had been gone. He must've slipped out in the night, when Brand had been fast asleep.

"Ready?" Kamoor stared at him as Brand stopped in front of him.

Brand only nodded, feeling dejected by the thought of his future prospects. He was all alone in the world, with no one to turn to. Khatlah, whom he at least considered to be a friend, was absent. He should've been there to say goodb—

"Brand!"

Brand turned slightly at the shout and found himself with an armful of Khatlah, who wrapped his arms around his neck and held fast tightly. Surprised at the sudden arrival and the tight embrace, Brand hesitantly wrapped his own arms around him.

He watched from the corner of his eye how Kamoor's neutral expression instantly turned into a scowl, but what really threw him was the satisfied smirk on Sakoptari's face.

"You better come back," Khatlah whispered into his ear. "You hear that? You better come back!"

He stepped back, arms falling away from Brand's shoulders. He turned to Kamoor next, glaring. "He better come back. If something happens to him— If any of you do something to him—" The warning was clear in his voice.

"We'll bring your lover back, do not worry," Sakoptari spoke up.

Khatlah looked at him, surprise evident in his face. Brand took in the smirk still on the crown prince's face, then looked at Kamoor, who was still scowling. Something was going on, something he was missing completely...

Kamoor's eyes suddenly cut to him, meeting Brand's gaze head on. "Get on," he ordered, motioning to his dragon.

Brand drew up short. "What?" He was not supposed to ride on that... was he?

"Get. On." Kamoor grabbed his arm, hauling him up to the dragon's side. It was geared up with something resembling a horse's saddle. Hesitating briefly, looking at the dragon's eyes as it turned its head to look at him, Brand climbed on.

Kamoor mounted in front of him, and Brand searched for somewhere else to hold on before he carefully inched his arms around Kamoor's waist. He turned his head, looking back down at Khatlah, who was looking up at them, face unreadable.

Kamoor said something in his native tongue, a short, sharp word that could only be an order, and the dragon stood up properly, jostling Brand flush up against Kamoor's back. Then it spread its wings, and moments later they were in the sky.

Brand had never thought about heights before, but then he had always been firmly on the ground. But... he was atop a dragon, far up in the sky, and he suddenly found himself clutching at Kamoor's side so hard he knew Kamoor would most likely have bruises there for days. But he could not let go, because he was terrified. He was not made for heights—he was made for being on the ground, for running around in the woods.

The dragon glided through the sky, the enormous, powerful wings only beating once in a while to keep it up. Brand found it was better to watch the wings than to look down below.

He did not know how long they were in the sky, but the dragon gradually started to move towards the ground. It landed hard on the ground, jostling Brand flush up against

Kamoor's back again.

Scrambling down off of the dragon's back, Brand turned to look at the woods and the mountains. It felt like it had been ages since last he had seen a tree, but he knew it really wasn't. The events of the last days only made it seem so.

"We set camp here, then head out to thoroughly canvass the woods," Kamoor spoke up.

Brand barely noticed as they moved around him, his eyes only for the mountains covered in woods. They were lush and green and reminded him so much of home... of the Fenris Forest, except the fact that it did not lay on a mountain.

"He did not leave your room last night."

Brand jerked in surprise at Kamoor's low voice coming from beside him. Turning his head, he watched Kamoor stare straight ahead, though Brand wasn't at all sure he was actually seeing the forest.

"He did not leave your room." Kamoor's jaw clenched tight and Brand could clearly see the feelings warring inside him.

Brand did not say anything. Kamoor had not been kind to Khatlah, after all, so why should Brand appease his mind? Let him believe something else had been going on inside that room, let him taste the jealousy.

Brand turned, seeing that they had set camp in the middle of what appeared to be the ancient ruins of some house or temple. Sakoptari was within earshot, but he did not look at them, and the other man was further inside the ruins.

Kamoor turned on his heel, still not looking at Brand. "Sakoptari, Sarab! You will scout the east, we will take the west side. We meet back here come nightfall."

Kamoor actually wanted to stay with him? Brand couldn't help but stare at him. Did he want to stay close, to keep an eye on Brand? Or was he going to torture himself by staying with Khatlah's supposed new lover? Or perhaps Brand would soon find himself very dead...

They parted ways, leaving the dragons behind to guard the camp. Brand did not know what to say, what to do as he suddenly found himself completely alone with Kamoor. At least before there had been two other men with them.

Kamoor's hard, dark eyes cut to him as they walked deeper into the woods. "What does he see in you?" he questioned sharply.

Brand averted his gaze. "I do not know. What does he see in you?"

Kamoor turned his head roughly away, his

jaw again clenching in anger. Brand couldn't help but feel a bit satisfied at that, but his smile did not last for long. Khatlah loved Kamoor, no matter how cruel he had been to Khatlah in the past...

"Do not mock me. You know nothing about what has happened before you arrived."

"I know that Khatlah spoke the truth to me last night," Brand replied. "No one can make a lie so convincing, of that I am certain. He was crushed yesterday, because of you. Crushed. He has been alone for so long, no one gives him the time of day anymore. He was kind to me when no one else was, so I owe it to him to help him."

"Help him?" Kamoor glared at him briefly before turning back to peruse the woods in front of him.

"Khatlah never betrayed you," Brand told him quietly. "So wherever you got that notion, it is wrong. All he ever wanted was you." Brand did not want to say the words, but he had to, for Khatlah. He quickened his steps, his boots crunching on the uneven ground of the forest, covered with grass, twigs and fallen leaves.

He could hear Kamoor following him, but he only increased his pace. Brand had lived in the forest all his life, while Kamoor was of the desert, and though he might be used to the treacherous ground of the woods, for Brand it was innate.

"Do not walk away from me, wolf!" Kamoor snapped. "You do not get to say such a thing and just walk away!"

"What more is there to say?" Brand replied tiredly.

"You do not know Khatlah. How can you know he speaks the truth?"

"I may not know him well, but when someone cries all over me, it generally means that person is speaking the truth!" Brand turned, glaring angrily at Kamoor. "Why can you not believe him? Who do you trust so much that you turn on the man you love?"

A stricken look flickered over Kamoor's face for just a moment before he managed to mask it. He clenched his jaw again, anger burning in his eyes, but Brand could see the difference in it. His anger was no longer towards Brand, or even Khatlah, but someone else.

"Let us be civil and do what we are here to do," he suggested, knowing that they would not get anything done if they continued to bicker. The ones they were there to find would hear them for miles—and they might run off, but most likely they would just kill them.

Kamoor's anger dimmed as his mind settled on what they were supposed to do. He nodded, and Brand flexed his fingers, his eyes roaming. As a human he knew forests, he had lived in them, but as a wolf he was part of the forest.

"Let us hunt." And so he shifted.

Brand used his powers to stoke the fire and watched the wood crackle. He could've made flames without the wood, but he did not want to constantly use his powers, because he did not want his eyes to constantly be the colour of the very flames he was looking at.

Kamoor was beside him, sitting on what appeared to be part of a fallen arch, and angrily carving on a piece of the wood they had brought from the forest. Brand did not have to look at him to see the anger and the tension, it was clear in his movements. It seemed to radiate from him. Night was starting to fall and they were waiting for Sakoptari and Sarab to come back.

Brand and Kamoor had not come across anything of interest in the forest, and had eventually returned to camp. The fact that the other two were not back yet gave Brand hope that they at least had discovered something.

Brand had not known the three men he had followed over the mountain had been a part of a bigger group. It did not surprise him, however. Those men had been scum and he had no doubt that the rest of the group was, too. He wanted them gone, because dragons were magnificent creatures that should not be killed in such ruthless ways.

"Do you name your dragons?" he questioned, breaking the heavy silence.

"Yes," was the short reply.

Brand looked up at the sky. The dragons had left once he and Kamoor had come back, though he did not know to where. "What is your dragon's name?" He couldn't help but be curious, dragons were as far from his life as was possible. They had been myth to him for all his life, and though he had gone searching for them... he had not actually thought he would see one.

"Atesh," Kamoor replied.

"Does it have a specific meaning?"

"Fire."

Brand turned towards Kamoor at that and found him looking right back at him. In the ancient language, Brand's name meant the exact same thing. He shared a name with Kamoor's eerie dragon—it was a coincidence, but a disconcerting one.

"I do not think your dragon likes me," he commented. "Though I should not be surprised. No one really does."

"Khatlah likes you," Kamoor replied, voice low.

Brand chuckled bitterly. "Not as much as he likes you." Really, when this was over, Brand had to get away from there. He'd have to travel north, towards the Jotun Territory, because he was soon all out of options.

Kamoor cleared his throat, but movement ahead brought his attention away from Brand. Brand saw Sakoptari and Sarab heading towards camp, silently walking next to each other. Brand could practically feel Kamoor's anger and tension return. Frowning, he did not even manage to turn his head before Kamoor was on his feet and stalking over to the two. He went right up to Sakoptari and swung his fist, catching the surprised prince on the side of his face.

Sakoptari went sprawling to the ground, but he quickly managed to get back on his feet and he stared with wide eyes back at Kamoor. "What is the matter with you?"

"You lied to me!" Kamoor snarled. "You are supposed to be my friend and you lied!"

Sakoptari looked completely bewildered, and Brand frowned even more. What was going on? Sarab looked completely out of it, too, keeping himself at a distance from the two friends.

"About Khatlah!" Kamoor yelled. "You told me—" He had to stop and swallow, obviously not getting the words out. "You lied!"

Sakoptari's confusion cleared. "You're bringing that up? That happened ages ago!"

"That does not matter because you still lied!" Kamoor swung again, but that time Sakoptari was more prepared and blocked it. They scuffled for several minutes, neither gaining the upper hand, until Kamoor stepped back with a snarl. "I trusted you," he got out through clenched teeth. "I trusted you and you went and ruined everything!"

He turned and stalked back to the camp, going past Brand without so much as a look and over to his sleeping pallet. Brand looked at his back for a moment, then turned to see what Sakoptari would do... and found Sakoptari's eyes burning with hate as they stared at Brand. Brand felt a tingling sensation going down his spine, but he did not back down from that stare.

So Sakoptari was the one who had ruined everything between Khatlah and Kamoor. But for what? The hate in his eyes could not possibly be for Brand—not to that extent. But then who did he hate? Khatlah? Or Kamoor himself?

When Sakoptari broke the gaze to go over to his own bed pallet, Brand breathed out. His eyes flickered to Sarab, who had crouched down on the other side of the fire. Sarab was not looking at him, or at the other two. Sighing, Brand lay down on his bed pallet, which he had moved next to the fire. Fire was his element and he wanted to be close to it.

Brand woke to a hand covering his mouth and a dagger pressed against his throat. He did not protest as he was being dragged to his feet and pushed towards the forest. He blinked the sleep from his eyes, letting his brain clear. It was still night, but dawn was near, and someone was holding him at knife point, and they did not want him to be able to call for help. Meaning that at least one man had to be back at the camp asleep, without knowing what was going on.

They reached the forest and Brand was

forced further in, before he was roughly shoved to the ground in the middle of a small clearing. Rolling over, Brand stared up at the one who had got the better of him. "Sakoptari." He glared, but stayed very still, not sure what to expect. Those dark eyes still burned with hate and rage.

"Who do you think you are?" Sakoptari snarled. "Coming here and turning Kamoor against me? I did not mind you going after Khatlah. All the better, I say, because that would for sure get him out of my face at every turn. But no, you come after Kamoor as well, and then tell him I am a liar!"

Brand was starting to see where the conversation was going. "You lied to Kamoor," he snapped. "You lied to him, thinking he would come to you in his grief, did you not?" The flickering of Sakoptari's eyes told him he was right. "You lied to him about your own brother!"

"Kamoor is mine!" Sakoptari yelled. "That little good-for-nothing is not worth the attention of Kamoor!"

"So you made sure he would never get it again," Brand commented, feeling his disgust with Sakoptari rise. Brand might've caused Garrick pain with his behaviour in the past, but he had never gone that far: he had never tried to take another chance at love away from him. He would never do such a thing. Garrick was happy with his witch, and Brand had had to move on. He would never sink so deep. "But Kamoor never came to you, did he?" He couldn't help but mock, because if Kamoor had ever gone to Sakoptari's bed, then Sakoptari would not react so violently.

Sakoptari pursed his lips angrily. "You came here a prisoner. I beat you up so badly that my weak brother took pity on you. You are nothing here. Nothing! So do not come here and ruin everything I am working on. Because I will kill you."

"If Kamoor hasn't come to your bed before, he will not now!" Brand told him angrily. "You cannot force someone to feel that way with lies and deceit. It does not work that way!"

"And how would you know?" Sakoptari stepped closer. "It got them apart and it has kept them apart for so long. Until you arrived. You have been a thorn in my side since we captured you. I should've just lodged my arrow in your chest from the beginning and I would not have to deal with this." He lunged, and Brand barely managed to roll over in time to avoid the sharp dagger.

He pushed to his feet and backed away, not knowing what to do. Should he just run? No, he could not do that, because then Sakoptari would go back to camp saying he had never been on their side after all, that when he had had the chance he had turned tail and run, and no one would know what Sakoptari had done. So Brand couldn't. He had to stay and try to keep himself alive.

"Why aren't you fighting back?" Sakoptari snarled.

"Because I cannot kill you," Brand replied, dodging another lash out. "You are the crown prince and no one will believe it was in self-defence if I were to kill you."

"Like you could kill me," Sakoptari yelled. "I am a warrior and you're just a lowly prisoner I beat up for the fun of it!"

Sakoptari was not sane, Brand realized. Not sane and certainly not fit to sit on any throne. Twisting away from another lash-out, Brand let his eyes roam the forest, looking for something to gain an advantage without having to kill Sakoptari. But in that moment Sakoptari saw his chance, and he was on Brand immediately, and they both fell to the ground in a flurry of arms and legs.

Brand called out in pain as the knife cut into his side, and when Sakoptari sat up he instantly moved his hands to try to stop the bleeding. Looking up at Sakoptari, who was straddling his waist, he saw that mad gleam in his eyes again as he held the dagger high above his head. Brand realized with horror that that dagger was going to be lodged right into his heart.

Sakoptari started to lower his hands and Brand saw it as if it happened much slower than it really did. He wanted to shift, but he would still be stuck. He wanted to use his powers but that would kill Sakoptari... and so he was destined to die by the hand of a madman.

Sakoptari jerked to a stop, the knife hovering inches above Brand's heart. He jerked again, and his eyes widened, then a sword was thrust through his abdomen, blood gushing out over Brand to mix with his own. Sakoptari was pushed off of him, and then Brand saw what had made him jerk — two arrows lodged in his back.

"Brand!"

Brand looked up at Kamoor, dazed by his own pain and the fact that his attacker had just been killed. Kamoor stood above him, frowning down at him for a moment before he crouched down. "Where?" he demanded, but Brand's clutching grip on his side gave him the answer. He pried Brand's hands away and ripped more of the tunic open so that he could get to the wound. "Why did he do this?" Kamoor asked, the pain of killing his best friend clear to Brand, even through his own physical pain.

"Because of you," he whispered. "Because he wanted you so badly... that he would get rid of everyone standing in his way."

A twig breaking had his head moving, but it was only Sarab joining them in the clearing, still holding his bow and arrow at the ready. But something still did not feel right and Brand pushed himself up in a sitting position.

"Stop that! You're disrupting the wound," Kamoor snapped, but Brand did not listen to him, instead letting his eyes roam the woods— listening, smelling, seeing—

"Get down!" He shoved Kamoor to the ground, and lay down atop him, hoping to keep him down as the arrows whistled above them. "They're here," he whispered, "the men we are hunting... They're hunting us." Brand stared into Kamoor's eyes as he spoke, noticing that they were such a deep brown that they almost appeared to be black. "But this I can deal with."

He pushed to his feet and let his power run through his body. He knew his eyes had already changed colour and held his hands slightly up and in front of himself, palms up, and let a ball of flame light up above each of them. An arrow came flying and Brand dodged it at the same time as he threw both balls of flame towards the place it had come from.

A person screamed, and at the same time the high bushes hiding him from sight caught fire. Brand used his senses to find another, and when he could both hear him move restlessly and smell him, he let another ball of flame go. That man screamed too, and again the ground consisting of leaves and grass and twigs caught fire.

A loud battle cry came from behind him, and Brand turned in time to watch as one of the dragon killers came charging into the clearing. Kamoor was on him before Brand could do anything, steel clashing against steel, the fight not even lasting a minute before Kamoor sliced him with his sword. The rest of the men, at least seven of them, came charging after. Two going towards Kamoor, two towards Sarab, and the remaining three towards Brand.

Brand backed up, leading his three opponents a safe distance away from Kamoor and Sarab, then used his powers to carve a burning circle in the ground around them, effectively shutting them away from the rest of the fight. Brand was confident that both Kamoor and Sarab could handle the men they were fighting.

One of the men inside the flames with him seemed to be panicking as he watched the wall of flames that kept him prisoner. Brand had never used his powers to kill before, nor had he used them to such an extent, but he wanted to see how far he could push them, and he concentrated hard, gathering all his power, then he released it on the three men in front of him before they could charge him. He watched as the flames consumed them.

When they fell to the ground, dead, he used his powers to withdraw the fire. The circle of flame dimmed, then disappeared completely, leaving only the burned, charred evidence of it in the ground. Brand saw that Kamoor had killed both his opponents, and Sarab killed the last one as he turned his gaze towards him. Brand turned his attention to the fire he had created in the woods, but a sound caught his attention.

Someone was running away.

chapter four
fire

Brand shifted immediately and sprinted after the man, jumping through the burning bush he had first set on fire. One dead man lay on the ground, his body badly burned, but the ground showed the footsteps of another, and he was loud in the woods as he ran away. Brand pursued, running after the sound of the man's boots crunching on dried leaves and breaking fallen twigs, and as he came closer he also heard the man's laboured breathing.

Brand was not letting one of them get away. His side ached, even in wolf-form, but he ran on, his focus solely on the pursuit.

The man came into sight, and Brand quickened his pace even more, pushing himself as far as he could go. When he got close enough he jumped, his paws digging into the man's back, making him loose his balance and fall face first to the ground.

He groaned in pain but his hand searched for the sword at his side. Brand snarled and locked his jaw around the man's lower arm, tearing the fabric and the flesh. He screamed.

"Brand!" Kamoor came running, his sword in one hand and a dagger in the other. He strode towards them, jaw set and eyes focused, and Brand stepped away, letting Kamoor do the job of killing the man.

Brand stumbled, and as he shifted back he found himself on his knees. He touched his side gently and his hand came away covered in blood. Looking down, he saw the blood oozing from his wound, and back in human form, the pain came rushing back, making him dizzy and nauseous.

"You should've left those men to me," Kamoor snapped, as he was suddenly at Brand's side. "Sarab and I would've handled them just fine. Now you have gone and made your wound a hundred times worse."

Brand could only laugh bitterly. "I have been hurt all my life," he revealed, "this is no different than being beaten daily, or being whipped or attacked by a lindworm. Do not

worry, Commander, I am perfectly used to this."
It was sad really, if he thought too much about
it.

But it was true. His injuries were nothing
compared to his father's sadistic ways to break
him. His father had not succeeded though,
because Brand had picked himself up and gone
after Garrick and that witch, and he had got to
his old friend just in time to divert a lindworm
from landing a fatal blow.

So being taken prisoner and beaten up was
nothing unusual for him, though it always hurt,
and being stabbed... he had never actually been
stabbed before, and it was something else
entirely than being whipped, but he could not
make up his mind on what hurt the most,
because both hurt greatly in their own ways.

Brand could take pain. He could take being
beaten. But the pain of a knife cutting open his
flesh... he was not good with that kind of pain.

"You should apologize to Khatlah," he
mumbled, slumping against Kamoor's bigger,
more muscular body. He knew he was going to
pass out: he had lost too much blood. Whether
he would wake again was another matter, so he
had to have his say. "You should just apologize
to him... and be happy together."

Then everything went black.

Brand woke to the crackling of a fire and he blinked his eyes open. It was dark, with the stars clear in the sky. The events of the day came back to him, and he closed his eyes again. He had been stabbed, Kamoor had been forced to kill Sakoptari and Brand himself had killed over half of the dragon slayers. He had never killed anyone before.

Breathing next to him brought his eyes back open, and he turned his head a fraction. Kamoor was asleep on a pallet at his side, his chest rising and falling slowly.

"You really frightened him," a quiet voice spoke up, and Brand turned his head to the other side to see Sarab crouching by the fire. "He has been by your bedside all day, watching, cleaning and wrapping your wound."

"What have you been doing?" Brand asked, watching the tired lines on Sarab's face.

"I've buried all those dead men in the woods," Sarab replied, stoking the fire with a stick. "They deserve a proper burial, no matter what they have done, and the people of your country are buried in the soil, are they not?"

"Yeah. We bury our dead." Brand bit his lip, both wanting to and not wanting to ask the question of Sakoptari. He needed to know the answer and at the same time he did not.

"Sakoptari will be transported back to the palace," Sarab answered his unvoiced question. "We are just waiting on a transport. We cannot take him on a dragon. Not you either, with that wound. So someone will come with a transport to bring you both back home."

"And what will happen once we get there?" Brand questioned, voice so low it was almost a whisper.

"Not anything good, I assure you. Kamoor killed the crown prince. There will be a hearing, at the least." Sarab's voice was neutral, but Brand caught the hint of uncertainty underneath it.

"He was not sane," Brand commented. "He wanted me dead because I told Kamoor of his lies. Lies that had ruined everything between Kamoor and Khatlah. Who knows what else he has been up to?"

Sarab bowed his head. "He has been up to a lot. But it does not change the fact that the crown prince is dead, and that the Commander of the dragon riders delivered the killing blow. I shot the arrows—so I will most likely be taken upon my return as well."

Sarab looked like he had direct knowledge of what else Sakoptari had been up too, but Brand did not want to pry into his personal business. "Taken where?" he asked instead.

Sarab smiled slightly. "To the dungeons."

"I have probably earned myself another stay there as well," Brand sighed, turning his head back to look at the stars.

"I would believe so, yeah." Sarab subsided into silence, and he stared into the fire for several moments longer before he finally stood up and went over to his own bed pallet.

Brand looked at Kamoor again. Sarab had said he had been frightened... and that he had stayed by Brand the whole day. Why? Why would he do that? Brand was the only one standing between Kamoor and Khatlah. So why should Kamoor care about what happened to him?

"Brand?"

Brand stayed put, but turned his head to look towards where Kamoor's voice came from. "Now you can talk to me?"

"Excuse me?" Kamoor sounded genuinely puzzled.

"All the way back here you could not be bothered to talk to me," Brand commented angrily. They had been seized immediately upon returning to the palace and placed in the dungeon. It had been a few hours, half a day at most. All three of them were in different cells, but Kamoor was in the one right next to Brand's.

"Get over here." Kamoor's voice was sharp and brooked no argument.

Brand got up, with a little difficulty due to his injury. Unable to see in the pitch-black darkness inside the dungeon, he let a small flame flicker to life in front of him. Kamoor stood at the bars and Brand walked up to stand in front of him, a small grunt of surprise escaping him as Kamoor grabbed a hold of his tunic and hauled him close.

"You have a very low opinion of yourself," he said, his voice low and intense. "But if you are used to being in pain, I understand why. You are an individual and each individual is special. I see what Khatlah sees in you. So you should raise that opinion you have, because you are special. No one here can shift to the form of the wolf-creature—and no one has the ability you have with fire."

"I am not particularly special, more peculiar," Brand told him snappishly, refusing to show how much Kamoor's manhandling hurt his wound. "A shifter is supposed to bond to a witch, not become one! I am not really complaining, because I think I would make a very poor bonded, but I am strange all the same."

"Stop it!" Kamoor hauled him in even closer, if that were possible. The cold iron bars dividing them cut into Brand's torso. "You should not speak of yourself like that."

"Why do you care?" Brand yelled, trying to fight Kamoor's hold on him, but Kamoor was too strong; he did not stand a chance.

"Because Khatlah wants you back!" Kamoor snarled. "I killed my best friend for you, to get you back here so that you could be with Khatlah."

"You should be with Khatlah," Brand told him. "I have cleared things up between you, so that you are free to be together. He loves you."

"He *loved* me," Kamoor said, grimacing as if he were in pain. "But he *loves* you. I ruined my chance with him—you better not do the same. Because if you hurt him, I will hurt *you*."

Kamoor pushed him away, and Brand stumbled back, only barely managing to stay on his feet. It pulled on his wound, and he groaned as he reached down to curl his arm around his waist.

Brand opened his mouth to speak, or yell, he did not know which, but the creak of the dungeon doors brought his attention away from the infuriating man in the other cell.

It was Khatlah. He held a torch high, and looked at all three of them, then he approached Brand's cell. "What happened out there?" he questioned, one hand reaching out to clutch at a bar. "Why is Sakoptari dead and you three held in the dungeon?" His eyes stared hard at Brand.

Brand bowed his head, not knowing what to say and not wanting to look into those intense eyes. Obviously Khatlah needed the truth—he had to know that it was his own brother who had been responsible for all the lies and deceit and hurt and anger. But he did not know how to tell him.

"Sakoptari tried to kill your lover, is what happened," Kamoor spoke up brusquely. "So I killed him."

Khatlah's eyes cut to Kamoor. "You killed your best friend for the man you believe to be my lover?"

Kamoor's face was as set in stone. "Yes, I did. Because he was not the friend I believed him to be. For years he's been lying to me—and I trusted him instead of the person I really should've trusted."

Khatlah eyes widened as realization struck. "You mean it was..."

Kamoor nodded.

"But why? Why would he do such a thing?" Khatlah was visibly upset, and Brand took several steps forward, wanting to comfort him, but knowing that he could not.

"Because he wanted Kamoor," he told him quietly. "He wanted Kamoor so badly he wrecked your relationship and when I told Kamoor that he had been lied to... Then Sakoptari went for me. If Kamoor hadn't killed him, I would be dead. He was not sane, Khatlah. He's been hiding it well, but he was not sane."

Khatlah listened to him in silence, then stood with his head bowed for a long time. When he raised it again he did not look at any of them. "I will speak to Father. He cannot let you stay down here, not considering you haven't really done anything wrong." And so he turned on his heel and stalked out, taking the light of the torch with him.

Brand sank to the floor once the door had creaked shut, weak from the trauma his body had gone through. He wrapped his arms around his legs, pulling them up against his chest. He rested his forehead against his kneecaps, his mind churning with everything that had happened. Everything he wanted to happen, but which he could no longer have, because Kamoor and Khatlah belonged together, and Brand was just an outsider.

He would have to leave. If the king ever let him out, that was. No matter what was decided, Brand was done. Completely done.

Brand groaned as he was forcefully shoved forward and down. Glancing to his side, he saw that the guards were decidedly more respectful towards both Kamoor and Sarab. They knelt on the floor without having to be forced down, and the guards had barely even touched them as they'd been guided them up into the palace proper.

They were in the audience chamber of the king. Brand dared a look up and saw a man, very plain looking, but decidedly related to both Khatlah and Sakoptari, sitting on a raised dais. A man he did not know, but who also must be related stood at his other side and on the other, the one closest to Brand, stood Khatlah. His dark eyes locked with Brand's for a moment and a tiny smile flickered across his lips for the briefest moment. Brand couldn't bring himself to smile back, because he did not know what that smile meant or even what was going to happen to him.

"My youngest son has told me of what transpired in the Border Mountains," the king spoke up. He related the tale they had told Khatlah in short, clipped words. "Is this true?"

"Yes, your majesty." Kamoor bowed his head. "Every word of it is true, I swear on my life and that of my dragon."

Sarab also bowed his head as the king looked his way. "I too swear on my life and that of my dragon that it is true."

The king's eyes turned to Brand last. "You are not of the desert," he said, pointing out the obvious. "And as such, your words hold no power here, but Commander Kamoor and Sarab are trusted men and I believe their word. They are cleared of all charges, as are you, but you are hereby banished from my land."

Brand closed his eyes as the verdict fell, taking it calmly.

"Father!" Khatlah exclaimed. "He has done nothing wrong!"

"He came here a prisoner, accused of slaying dragons," the king argued.

"But he did not!" Khatlah yelled. "You cannot banish someone who hasn't done anything wrong! That is unjust!"

"Why are you standing up for an outsider?" The king's voice was rising as well, anger spilling through. "You know how we feel about outsiders, Khatlah! The ones we have let into our fold we have done so with utmost care. You know nothing about this man!"

"No one can know everything there is to know about someone!" Desperation was clouding Khatlah's voice and Brand looked up at him in surprise. Why would Khatlah fight for him like this? "But I do know that this man has never hurt a dragon and I know he helped Commander Kamoor get rid of the slayers, which is our greatest threat! He helped, Father! I also know that he has no one and no home to go to! So if anyone we have ever let in deserves to stay here, he does!"

"Your son is right," Kamoor spoke up, and he rose smoothly to his feet, facing the king. "Brand has been a great help. His special abilities were the only reason we managed to get all those men. Perhaps the only reason both me and Sarab are still alive. Those men hunted us, and they would've got us if it hadn't been for Brand. I use my right as commander of the dragon riders to vote for him being allowed to stay."

Khatlah sent Kamoor a look Brand could not quite decipher before turning back to his father. "Please, Father... Let him stay."

The king stared hard at Kamoor, and Kamoor met his gaze straight on. "I trust your judgment, Commander. If you say this man is to be trusted I will take you at your word. He is allowed to stay."

Khatlah let out a relieved sigh, then in a flurry of movement he jumped down off the dais and embraced Brand tightly, burrowing his face against Brand's neck. Brand could see Kamoor looking at them from the corner of his eye, but he turned away without a word. Brand felt sorry for him, for he knew that Kamoor still loved Khatlah, but at that moment he couldn't care less, because Khatlah was clinging to him, like no one ever had, and it felt good, and Brand could not help but wrap his own arms around Khatlah's waist, bringing him closer, tighter. The wound in his side throbbed, but not even that could trouble him.

All that mattered was that he was actually allowed to stay, and that Khatlah was hugging him in joy. The thought of actually leaving had already flown from his mind, replaced by nothing but happiness.

"What is it about this man that kept you alive, Commander?" the king questioned. "He does not have the look of a warrior. You could've easily bested him."

"I could," Kamoor agreed, "if you only look at what you see on the outside, but this man has something special about him... something that gave us quite the advantage in the woodlands."

"And what is that?" The king bent forward in his seat, his voice demanding an answer.

Khatlah pulled back a little so that he could turn his head to watch his father, but he stayed very close to Brand and his arms did not unwind completely from around his neck.

"If you have noticed his strange eyes, they are the eyes of the wolf-creature that lives in the woods," Kamoor told him. "He is able to shift his form into that of the wolf-creature, and as such his senses are much better than ours. He is also able to create and manipulate fire with his mind, and when he does that, his eyes change to the colour of flames."

The king's eyes cut from Kamoor to Brand. "You really can create flames? Show me."

Brand did not even think about disobeying the order. The king had just allowed him to stay, and as such he deserved to know what Brand was. Brand lifted his hand and flipped it over, curling his fingers up as he called forth a small ball of flame. It hovered above his palm, and the flames played around Brand's fingers, hot to the touch to anyone but him.

"That is remarkable." The king leaned back, one hand going to his chin as he regarded Brand.

"Father..." Khatlah's voice was full of warning. "Whatever it is you're planning right now, this is not the time or the day for it."

The king sobered at the reminder. "You are right, my son. Another day, then." He nodded to each of them in turn. "You are all dismissed. Except Khatlah."

"I'll be out soon," Khatlah whispered to Brand. "I'll come find you."

Brand turned and exited the audience chamber alongside Kamoor and Sarab.

"Care to join us on the roof?" Kamoor glanced at him briefly.

Brand only nodded, following the two men silently.

Without Khatlah pressed up against him his mind was once again thinking clearly—and it was doubting, but he was going to take things as they came, at least until his wound had healed.

They emerged on the roof to the most beautiful view Brand had ever seen. The sun was setting in the horizon, leaving the land in an orange glow.

He watched Kamoor and Sarab approach their dragons, greeting them with a clap to their necks. Besides the injured youngling that lay curled up across the roof, those two were currently the only dragons there.

"Where is Sakoptari's dragon?" Brand asked the question hesitantly, but he was curious about what happened to a dragon when their rider died.

"Her rider is dead. She has no ties here anymore. She's gone." Sarab was the one to answer, and he sounded genuinely sad about it. "It is quite sad, because she was a fine dragon."

"Does a dragon only have one rider in a lifetime?" Brand questioned quietly.

"Some choose a second rider. It depends on how the first rider dies and how well the dragon can handle that death. Not being able to be ridden by your rider ever again... it is hard on the dragons. Just like it is hard on us to lose a loved one."

Brand nodded that he'd heard, not knowing what to reply because it sounded like Sarab knew what it was like to lose a loved one. When he looked over at Kamoor Brand saw that Kamoor was staring at Sarab in surprise.

Kamoor had been quiet through it all, not saying a single word, and Brand felt his gut squeeze. Kamoor had lost one loved one, and he had no chance to reclaim the other one because Brand was stealing him away.

Turning away from them, Brand went over to the injured youngling. It lay quietly as he sat down next to it, but it was awake. One big, yellow eye looked at him. Brand placed one hand on the dragon's hind leg, splaying his finger over the hard, white scales.

"She'll be colouring soon," Kamoor spoke up from above him.

Brand looked up at him, surprised Kamoor had even followed him. "Colouring?"

"Younglings are always white," Kamoor explained, crouching down to stroke the dragon over the muzzle. "They do not colour until they reach the first stage of adulthood, though in bright sunlight they shimmer, like they are all colours at the same time. But they will not decide upon a colour until they become an adult."

"And when will that be?" Brand questioned.

"When they are ready to mate." Kamoor stroked down the dragon's neck. "This one should've coloured by now, she's big to be a youngling. But sometimes they take their time, just like humans. She doesn't know what she wants or who she wants."

"What do you mean by that?" Brand asked curiously.

"Dragon's mate for life. It is a complicated process to find a life-mate, because they have to be a complete match. They have to even each other out, and it is not easy to know who you are when you are just a youngling with no colour." Kamoor gently navigated his fingers in-between the spikes going down the youngling's spine. "She is hurt still, but when she's healed... She'll be on her way."

"She'll leave, just like that?" Brand did not like that. He felt attached to the dragon, though he could not really say why. She was the first dragon he had ever seen, so perhaps that was the reason.

"They all leave eventually, unless they bond with a rider." Kamoor's hands went over to carefully check the bandages.

"Who is your dragon's mate?" Brand asked, his eyes going to the enormous red beast standing across the roof.

"No one." Kamoor did not look up from the bandages. "He coloured early, but he never mated. It is a rare occurrence—but then Atesh is a rare dragon."

The dragon of the commander. That was rare—but Brand did not think that was what Kamoor was talking about.

The door leading up to the roof opened and closed, grabbing Brand's attention. Khatlah stepped out on the roof, his light clothing and head-cloth easily recognizable. He had caught Kamoor's attention as well, and Kamoor stared at him until Khatlah turned their way. Then Kamoor stood up, and with a nod to Brand he turned and stalked back to his dragon.

Khatlah glanced at him briefly before looking back at Brand, a small smile tugging at his lips as he approached.

"Did it go well with your father?" Brand asked worriedly. He stood up and waited for

Khatlah to reach him.

"Yes." Khatlah stopped only inches from him, just so that they barely touching. "He showed some concern for me when it comes to you, but I assured him that I am perfectly capable of living my own life."

Brand sobered right up at that. "You shouldn't be with me," he told him quietly. "You should be with Kamoor."

Khatlah turned serious as well then and he turned slightly to cast a look at Kamoor. "I loved Kamoor," he said, voice just as quiet as Brand's. "A small part of me always will, but there is too much anger, resentment and bitterness between us that will never go away, so the best we can hope for is to become friends." He turned back to Brand, dark eyes sincere. "I do not want Kamoor anymore. All I want is you, Brand. I love you. It might be early to say it, considering we only met days ago, but there it is. I love you and I want to be with you and I am under the impression that you want to be with me, too, unless I am sorely mistaken?"

Brand felt his gut squeeze tight, in a way both painful and thrilling, but the beat of powerful wings brought his attention over Khatlah's shoulder. They watched as Sarab's green dragon rose into the sky, followed by Kamoor's red one, both with their riders atop them. The wind created by those powerful wings hit them hard, making Brand's red hair fly around his face. It also disrupted Khatlah's head-cloth, and Brand could see a lock of dark hair inside.

The dragons rose quickly in the sky and soon glided away, leaving Brand and Khatlah alone on the roof with the injured youngling. Brand turned his gaze back to Khatlah, who was already looking up at him. "You are not mistaken," he whispered. "Not at all."

A smile slowly spread on Khatlah's lips again and he took the last step, bringing himself flush up against Brand. His hands travelled up Brand's chest and finally settled on the back of his neck. "You need a new start in life, as do I. We can move on together," Khatlah murmured, leaning in closer. "We can make a new life for ourselves right here, or anywhere, for that matter. I just want to be with you. You have brightened up my life like you wouldn't believe, like no one ever has."

Brand bent down the rest of the way, catching Khatlah's plump lips in a hard, passionate kiss. He wrapped his own hands around the back of Khatlah's neck, feeling the soft fabric of the head-cloth against his palm.

Breaking away entirely too early, he fiddled with the fabric against his hands. "Why do you always wear this?" he questioned. No one else he saw ever wore a head-cloth at all times, especially not inside the palace.

"It is a sign of mourning," Khatlah revealed, "to wear it at all times. At Sakoptari's funeral pyre tonight everyone will be wearing one, and they will wear them for three days straight."

"But you have worn yours since I first saw you," Brand commented. "You were not in mourning then."

"Yes, I was." Khatlah smiled bitterly. "I have been wearing this since the day I lost Kamoor. I have been in mourning ever since... but I am not anymore, not after I met you, so I guess it is finally time to take it off." He reached up with both hands and pulled the head-cloth back and down, then reached behind his neck and fished out a long, tightly braided plait.

The braid easily reached the small of Khatlah's back and the hair was a dark shade of auburn. Brand reached out, not really thinking about he was doing, and wrapped the end of the braid around his hand, his thumb stroking the soft hair. He wanted to take off the band holding the braid together, wanted to tangle his hand in the loose strands, but he knew Khatlah must spend quite some time on all that hair, so he settled for the braid.

He pulled Khatlah close again, wrapping his other arm around his waist. "Yes, I guess it is time." He kissed Khatlah again and that time he did not immediately pull back—he just kept kissing him until they were both out of breath. Brand rested his forehead against Khatlah's and they laughed, both happy and nervous at the same time.

A second later they found themselves sprawled on the ground, and Brand looked up at the youngling dragon getting to her feet. Her spreading wings were what had knocked them over. The youngling dragon beat her wings and Brand had to duck further down, pressing Khatlah down with him to avoid being hit.

The dragon reared up on her hind legs and she started to shimmer brightly. Brand watched, eyes wide, as the shimmer gradually was replaced by colour—starting at her muzzle and going all the way down her body to the tip of her tail. A colour greatly resembling Khatlah's hair...

The dragon turned her head and looked hard at Brand for several moments, then she beat her wings and rose. Brand scrambled to his feet, stared up at the underside of her belly as she rose high, and then she quietly glided away in the exact opposite way Kamoor and Sarab had gone. Khatlah got to his feet as well, standing close to Brand.

"She just... coloured," Brand muttered, watching her get further and further away.

"Remarkable." Khatlah sounded just as awed. "I have never seen a dragon colour before. It was... I do not have words for it."

Brand tilted his head back down towards Khatlah. He ran his hand gently over Khatlah's hair and gripped the end of the braid as he reached it. "It was the colour of your hair."

Khatlah let out a choked laugh. "It was not. You are seeing things."

Brand smiled slightly. "I can see better than you in the dark. It was the colour of your hair." Brand kissed him before Khatlah could once more protest.

Khatlah relaxed into the kiss, arms going around Brand's shoulders. Brand held him close and in that moment he never wanted to let go. He would be content to stay there on the roof, kissing Khatlah forever. For once he was master of his own life, and he had tried to give Khatlah an out... but Khatlah had not taken it, because Khatlah wanted him back, and so Brand was never going to let him go.

They did not know each other well, but they had the rest of their lives to figure it all out. Brand did not doubt for a second that they had that long... because Khatlah had proved that he did not stop loving easily by pining for Kamoor for such a long time — and Brand knew that neither did he.

about the author

TR lives in Scandinavia and likes to write fantasy stories with elements drawn from Scandinavian mythology. The stories are often sweet, with some drama and action, and sometimes steamy.

TR enjoys to read, write books, and listen to music. It's not often TR writes fantasy anymore, but a new story can pop up whenever inspiration strikes.

You can find TR Rook on Facebook here:
https://www.facebook.com/TR-Rook-698367826970993/